Daniel wanted to taste her...badly

She reached up, feathering her fingers over his lips. Risa couldn't read him, he realized with no small bit of relief—if she could she wouldn't be getting this close to him right now. Not with what he was thinking.

"It was my first one, you know," she murmured.

"First what?" He'd lost track. He was a CIA operative who'd been in hundreds of life-and-death situations, taken on missions that made action movies look like comic books, and yet here he was undone by a woman's touch.

"My first kiss."

"One worth repeating..." Daniel went in slowly this time, the light from the neon bar giving her an almost otherworldly glow. Her hair was like silk, and he closed his eyes at the erotic softness of it. Her lips were parted, asking him to hurry, but he was going to take his time and pleasure her.

When he finally took Risa's mouth she tasted of strawberries...and sheer female lust. She leaned into him again in that soft pliable way that made him instantly hard. Her kiss drove him to imagine what she'd be like naked, underneath him, and the desire to find out was so sharp he groaned....

Dear Reader,

I've always loved superheroes. *Superman,*
Buffy the Vampire Slayer and the *X-Men* are my
absolute favorites. These fascinating, often dark,
conflicted characters have always teased my
imagination. They've definitely influenced how I
create my own heroes and heroines.

When I got the chance to write an Extreme Blaze
novel, I was so excited to be able to create a
superhero of my own. What would it be like to have
superpowers? Then I thought, what would it be like
if you had them and then *lost* them? With this
thought, Risa Remington (superheroes always have
alliterative names!) was created. Superhero stories
also tend to revolve around a common theme: while
superpowers may be extraordinary, humanity really
saves the day. And what's more human, and more
powerful, than falling in love?

Feel free to e-mail me at
samhunter@samanthahunter.com or come by
the Harlequin Blaze boards at eHarlequin.com
to let me know what you think of Risa and Daniel's
story. You can also check out my Web site,
www.samanthahunter.com, to read updates
on new releases, contests, and more.

Sincerely,

Samantha Hunter

UNTOUCHED
Samantha Hunter

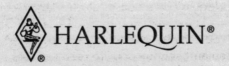

HARLEQUIN®

TORONTO • NEW YORK • LONDON
AMSTERDAM • PARIS • SYDNEY • HAMBURG
STOCKHOLM • ATHENS • TOKYO • MILAN • MADRID
PRAGUE • WARSAW • BUDAPEST • AUCKLAND

ISBN-13: 978-0-373-79303-7
ISBN-10: 0-373-79303-0

UNTOUCHED

This edition published by arrangement with Harlequin Books S.A.

® and TM are trademarks of the publisher. Trademarks indicated with
® are registered in the United States Patent and Trademark Office, the
Canadian Trade Marks Office and in other countries.

www.eHarlequin.com

Printed in U.S.A.

ABOUT THE AUTHOR

Samantha Hunter lives in Syracuse, New York, where she writes full-time for Harlequin Books. When she's not plotting her next story, Sam likes to work in her garden, quilt, cook, read and spend time with her husband and their dogs. *Untouched* marks her seventh Harlequin Blaze novel to date. Her first was *Virtually Perfect*, released in 2004. Most days you can find Sam chatting on the Harlequin Blaze boards at eHarlequin.com, or you can check out what's new, enter contests, or drop her a note at her Web site, www.samanthahunter.com.

Books by Samantha Hunter

HARLEQUIN BLAZE

*The HotWires

My thanks to Birgit, my superheroine editor, for giving me the chance to write this very special book.

Prologue

"CARE FOR A SCOTCH?"

Daniel MacAlister stood by the window looking out at the rainy suburban landscape of Bethesda. While not as romantic as the spy rendezvous on foggy London bridges and deserted parks that happened in movies, Jack White's Maryland town house served its purpose, and more comfortably. CIA field operatives—especially deep-cover ones like Daniel—didn't have offices, but worked all over the globe on assignments that rarely made the papers. A coded phone call would summon him when he was needed.

Daniel couldn't count how many times he'd stood in this spot, awaiting his orders. Jack always asked him if he wanted a drink, and Daniel always answered the same way. Jack's offer was a gesture, a pro forma nicety that Daniel wasn't expected to accept.

"No, thanks."

"All right then, down to business."

Jack took a folder from the black leather case on the desk and pushed it across the table, his voice matter-of-fact. "This is beyond top secret—destroy it when you're done."

The file, heavy in his hand, was as thick as a novel.

Daniel frowned. "Remington? I thought she was decommissioned after the accident last year."

Almost a year ago, Daniel had been infiltrating a secret terrorist lab discovered in the heart of the Nevada desert, with Risa Remington at his side. She wasn't an agent—she was the government's secret weapon, a mind-reading superhero. She'd lost her powers when something set off an electromagnetic blast in the lab—almost killing her, as well.

Jack took a leisurely sip of his drink, his sharp blue eyes meeting Daniel's, revealing nothing. "That's true. But she's not adjusting to civilian life. We're worried about her."

"She's become a threat?" he asked bluntly.

Jack shrugged. "We knew it was possible. But in spite of what people think, we're not in the habit of killing someone just because they're not useful to us anymore. We had to assume she'd stay quiet about everything she knows until she proved otherwise. She and her family have done a lot of good for this country. We owed her that chance, at least."

"But you think she's turning?"

"Uncertain. She's exhibiting questionable behaviors. Isolating herself in her apartment, using her Internet aliases and underground contacts to get her hands on basic surveillance equipment. She's emotionally unpredictable, unconnected to anyone in the real world, and she doesn't have any experience with normal, everyday life. It's been months since she went out on her own. We did what we could to help, but…"

"Why didn't you just keep her here?"

"Maintaining her life here was expensive. The government couldn't justify spending that amount of money to house a weapon that no longer works."

Daniel had worked with Risa Remington a half dozen times over the years. In spite of Jack's impersonal reference, Risa *was* human, an intensely beautiful woman, yet she didn't seem real. Maybe it was convenient for everyone, including him, to think of her as not quite human. It was a disturbing thought.

All agents were strictly ordered not to touch Risa—she could read thoughts, emotions, secrets, even physical statistics like blood pressure or heartbeat, with the slightest touch. Daniel had broken the no-touch protocol to go back and pull her out of the lab. He hadn't been reprimanded for his actions. After all, Risa was a valuable asset. At least, she had been.

Now she was on her own.

Daniel looked at Jack squarely. "What do you want me to do?"

"Make contact. Get inside. Basic recon—find out if she's into anything she shouldn't be. If she isn't, then perhaps you can help her make a more successful adjustment."

"I don't understand."

"Help her live in the normal world. Neutralize the potential for future threat."

Daniel's back stiffened, but his voice was calm. "You must be joking. Half the world is exploding out there and you want me to babysit?"

Jack finished the Scotch in one toss. "This is highly sensitive work—Risa is a special case, you know that more than anyone. You're familiar—she'll respond to you better than a stranger."

"I doubt that. We never spoke, except for what needed to be said on a mission. She had no idea who took her out of that lab. I never saw her afterward."

Jack's features relaxed, dismissing Daniel's objections with a wave of the hand. "You grew up in Falmouth. Lovely area. You have family there, right?"

Daniel nodded abruptly, not liking one bit where this was going. He wasn't about to discuss his family with Jack, although there was probably little the CIA supervisor didn't already know. He could follow Jack's logic. From the CIA's perspective, Daniel was the perfect choice. He knew Cape Cod like the back of his hand, had grown up there. Daniel, better than anyone, could help Risa acclimate to the community without raising suspicion. If he were inclined to do that. Which he wasn't, and he didn't bother to hide the fact.

Jack's tone was cajoling, but Daniel detected the steel underneath it. He wasn't being given a choice; it wasn't his job to argue.

"C'mon Daniel. You go home for a while. You blend in, get to see your family. It's been awhile, hasn't it? You keep an eye on Risa, maybe become a friend of sorts, maybe more, who knows? She's a beautiful girl, and she's never had any experience with men. Get as close as necessary to get the job done. Report back to us within six weeks, and if there are any signs of her having turned…" Jack's gaze met Daniel's as he delivered his final order. "You remove the threat. Permanently."

1

"HALLOOO? Risa? I have your groceries…*halloooo?*"

Risa Remington glared at the wide-screen monitor that covered the surface of her small desk. She'd taped a check onto the door as a not-so-subtle hint for her neighbor just to leave the groceries there, but Kristy was getting more insistent about seeing Risa face-to-face.

Risa watched Kristy, who stood clearly in the path of the hallway video feed. If she didn't open the door, Kristy would probably think something was wrong and get help. That was a hassle Risa just didn't need. She was trying to keep a low profile, intent on drawing as little attention as possible to herself until she could form some plan for her life.

Plan. Right.

She'd been stuck in this hole of an apartment in this hole of a town for six months. She had no plan but surviving day-to-day.

She looked at the perky young woman on the monitor, her streaked blond hair twisted up into a fun ponytail bound by something pink and fuzzy, her clothes sporty and equally colorful. Risa ignored the twinge of envy that settled in her gut. She didn't know how to be that kind of girl—pretty, lighthearted, carefree. She didn't know how to be a girl, period. Her life had been about much more important things than pink sweaters and kicky highlights. Risa didn't belong to that world—she had no idea what world she belonged in.

Maybe none.

Until she figured it out, she was staying put and depending on her neighbors' willingness to help out their new "agoraphobic" tenant. Thank goodness for popular TV series like *Monk* that made it commonplace to be a phobic personality. It worked like a charm. She didn't have to leave her apartment for anything; she didn't have to talk to anyone. Until now.

It was obvious that Kristy wasn't leaving until Risa opened the door. She had to be at least marginally friendly to the woman who'd brought her groceries. There was chocolate pudding in that bag. The only thing that was great about being off the government payroll was that now Risa could eat whatever she wanted. Her favorite thing was chocolate pudding. She could live on the stuff.

She opened the door as Kristy's hand was poised midair to knock yet again. Risa forced a smile and a hurried excuse that were both lies.

"I'm so sorry, Kristy—I was in the bathroom and didn't hear you. Are those mine? Thanks. I appreciate you doing this."

Reaching for the very full grocery bag, she hoped to duck back in, but Kristy wasn't so easily thwarted.

"I thought maybe you'd like some company. Today's

my day off, and I picked up some warm bagels at the bakery—do you have coffee?"

Kristy moved forward, comfortable with inviting herself in, apparently. More from reflex than anything, Risa's arm shot across the doorway, blocking Kristy's progress in a clear warning not to continue. When Kristy frowned, catching her eye, Risa forged another smile, and another lie.

"I'm sorry. Again. I just really have a lot of work to do today."

"You said you're a writer?"

"Yes. Technical. Freelance manuals for televisions, stoves, you know, that kind of thing. Nothing interesting. Nothing they put my name on."

Kristy looked nonplussed. "Oh. Well. I just thought, you know, since you never get out that you might like someone to come in and chat for a while. I read on the net that agoraphobics like company, they just don't like public places."

Risa clamped her teeth together, pushing down her irritation at Kristy's insistence. Her head was starting to hurt—the horrible headaches she'd had since the accident were fewer, but still intense—and her patience was wearing thin.

"Really, I just have so much work, but thanks…."

Tugging the heavy bag from Kristy's arms and nodding toward the check still taped to the door, Risa started to turn away, annoyed that she'd have to find another way to get her groceries. Kristy was getting far too nosy.

"Hey, are you okay?"

Kristy's voice seemed far away as Risa leaned against the door, the heavy bag disappearing from her arms as her knees turned to water. She heard a moan, probably her own, but as usual, when the headaches hit, she lost control completely. She didn't even feel the floor as she slumped, her body numb, her mind vaulting into another place, and she was powerless to stop it....

"A PUPPY!" Risa cried out joyfully as the tiny chocolate Lab ran in a crooked line, its oversized paws sliding on the slippery floor as it made its way to her. She picked up the soft, brown bundle and nestled it close, looking up at her mom with great hopes that the puppy was not just a temporary visitor.

"Is he mine? Can I name him?"

"Absolutely, honey. He's yours to keep. But you have to be very careful with him. He's just a baby and will need a lot of love and training."

"I promise. His name is Buddy."

Her mother stepped back, looking at Dr. Laslow, who stood to the side, smiling, too.

"Dr. Laslow! I have a puppy!"

"I see that, Risa. Good for you. Now, can you tell me what his stats are?"

Her mother's smile turned into a frown; Risa knew her mom didn't like it when Dr. Laslow asked her to tell him things, but Risa didn't mind. It was even kind of fun showing off her special powers.

Risa ran her small hands over the puppy's silky coat, warm, happy feelings cascading through her. She answered the doctor's question very clearly. "His heart-beat is one hundred seventy-five beats each minute, and his temperature is one hundred and one. He's healthy." She smiled, looking up for the doctor's approval.

"That's great, Risa. Can you tell me anything else about Buddy?"

"He's happy. He likes me," she announced with utter certainty and no small amount of pride. She couldn't read the animal's thoughts in the way she could a person's, but she could pick up on its physical and emotional state.

"Uh-oh."

"What, honey?" Her mother stepped forward, concerned.

"Buddy feels funny…he's very excited. I think he has to *go*."

She put the puppy down and sure enough, Buddy piddled immediately. Risa looked up, worried that the adults would be angry and take Buddy away. But her mom just smiled, reassuring her everything was fine. Dr. Laslow was too busy writing something in his notebook to notice. Her mom was saying something to her, and she listened closely, but she couldn't quite hear…it wasn't making sense….

"Risa. You're okay. Just rest a minute."

Opening her eyes, Risa stared at the blank, off-white stucco of her apartment ceiling, interrupted by Kristy's very concerned expression as she leaned over and looked down into Risa's face.

"What did you say?"

"You passed out. You must not have eaten enough this morning, had a blood sugar dip. Are you hypoglycemic by any chance?"

"No. You can go. I'm fine."

Kristy knelt by where Risa lay on the floor, putting a hand to Risa's forehead, much in the way Risa's mother used to do, and pushed her hair back.

"I'll just stay with you for a while. Make sure you're okay."

Risa pulled back—she didn't like being touched. The dream was still too fresh, the reality too sharp. When Kristy touched her she felt…nothing. Touching just reminded her of how cut off she was, how much she'd lost. It had taken her months to get used to using her computer manually; she felt cut off there, too, but had managed it. People were a different story.

A mere touch once told her everything she had needed to about the world and the people around her. Now she could see nothing. The constant blankness induced a sharp anxiety she couldn't bear. It reminded her of when she had touched her parents after their deaths, frantically running her hands over their faces searching for some connection, seeking some thought or memory, but there'd been nothing. They were blank, cold—gone from her.

The flashback played before her eyes again. Buddy had been with her for years, her best friend. Her *only* friend. She hadn't had another pet since he died when she was fourteen, ten years after he'd skidded across the floor into her arms. She still felt the pinch of losing him around her heart.

"I said I'm fine."

She stood up, putting distance between herself and Kristy, heading for the door to make it clear she wanted Kristy to leave.

"Fine, I'll go, but I'd like to know something first."

"What's that?" Risa shoved her fingers through her hair, impatient and anxious. Something had changed in the room, something was different about Kristy, her posture, her expression, but Risa couldn't tell exactly what it was. She didn't like being at such a disadvantage. She could sense something about Kristy's mental state, but it wasn't solid—like when a word you needed was just beyond your reach.

Kristy crossed her arms over her chest. "I'd like to know why you have a folder here with my name on it that tells you everything from what schools I attended to what men I date and what medicines are in my bathroom cabinet."

Risa froze. Kristy must have snooped while she was unconscious. Her mind raced for what to say, how to cover the truth, but Kristy filled in the silence between them.

"I was looking for a doctor's number when you passed out, a phone book or something with some information, and I found your files. I saw the hallway on your computer screen—you're monitoring everyone in the building, aren't you?"

Kristy pinned Risa with a shrewd gaze. "I'm guessing you're not agoraphobic, either. Are you law enforcement? Is there something dangerous going on here? I want to know. Do you want to tell me exactly why you're doing all of this, and how, or do I call the police and have them ask you?"

What the hell could she say? Kristy wouldn't believe the truth—would she?

Risa's urge to connect with someone, anyone, warred with her instinct to protect herself. She also hadn't forgotten her duty to keep top secret information secret. Her former life was as top secret as it got.

As Kristy stood staring at her, Risa thought maybe she could tell her something—a version of the truth, if not the truth itself. She'd been watching Kristy for months—there was nothing to suggest she was untrustworthy, and Risa didn't want the police digging around. Dr. Laslow had warned her about keeping a low profile. She had a normal life now, whatever that meant, but she still had to protect her past. Her powers might have disappeared, but all of the things she knew and witnessed hadn't. As Kristy reached for the phone again—to dial 911, no doubt—Risa stepped forward, putting up a hand in a halting motion.

"Please, don't call the police. I'll tell you what's going on." She tried a smile, knowing her attempt was lame. "Did you say you brought bagels?"

AN HOUR LATER, the bagels sat cold in the center of the kitchen counter, uneaten. Risa's appetite had faded and Kristy was listening with such rapt attention she'd forgotten to eat.

"I can't believe this—are you *serious?* You worked for the government as a psychic? You could read people's minds?"

"Yes, most of my life. My parents, too. And my grandfather. He approached the government in 1941, to help with the war effort. He felt it was his duty. He was already married and had my mother, who inherited the same ability, and then that was passed on to me. My father was a CIA agent, a regular guy. He met my mother back before…"

Risa drifted off. She couldn't tell Kristy that, after her mother and father's romance Dr. Laslow had made sure no such contact would be made with Risa. He'd said there was too much risk involved, too much access to secrets concerning Risa's powers. She cleared her throat and just skipped the subject altogether.

"Since then, our family has worked for the government, secretly, of course."

"Well, Reagan used to consult astrologers, I heard, and he took a lot of flack for that. So I can understand why they wouldn't want to let the media know they used professional psychics—and back to World War II even! But you don't have any powers now?"

Risa shook her head, relieved to be able to tell the truth on that, at least. She'd figured explaining her former abilities as psychic ones would be easier for Kristy to understand, without giving away too much. In reality, Risa wasn't a psychic, though her abilities had paralleled what some psychics claimed to be able to do. People talked about psychics all the time; it was a useful, harmless comparison that would serve its purpose.

Unlike psychics, who were a more paranormal phemonemon, Risa had inherited a supercharged nervous system that was physically differently than any normal human's. She could link with anything that held an electrical charge—man, animal or machine. She didn't operate on what she "felt" or on vague images, as psychics did.

She couldn't find dead bodies through dreams or pieces of clothing, though she could tell you exactly where a killer buried his victims just with a touch. Risa was hardwired to become part of what she touched. But it was best to keep her secrets, for Kristy's own protection, as well as anything else. In spite of her lack of abilities, there were still nefarious people who might be interested in "studying" her.

"Yes, they're all gone, so now I'm trying to lead a normal life. But I lived on government compounds since I was born—"

"Like an army brat?"

"Yeah. Like that. My parents died on a mission when I was five, and I was raised by the staff we worked with. I haven't known anything else. Ever."

Kristy's eyes welled up, and she reached across the table just as Risa drew her arm out of reach of the comforting touch. "That's just awful. You poor thing."

"I liked it, mostly. I helped people. What I did was important."

"And you've had these blackouts since your accident?"

Risa nodded. "They're supposed to go away in time. That's what Dr. Laslow said."

"He's your physician?"

"He was the doctor who took care of me since I was born. My mother, too."

Kristy sat back, clearly astounded and processing the information. "I can't imagine—you went on missions? Like a real spy?"

"Sort of. I was never really trained as a spy. They just needed me to ask people questions, you know, to find out information."

It had, of course, been much more involved than that, but she'd already said more than she should, and was feeling anxious about her revelations. Risa had been trained to keep secrets, but it seemed the point of "girl talk" was to tell all, something she wasn't free to do.

"So, you know all kinds of top secret stuff?"

Risa shifted uncomfortably. "Some. But you know the old line. If I told you about it, I'd have to kill you."

Kristy smiled at the cheesy joke, and shook her head in amazement. "I still don't understand about the files and the video—why do you monitor everyone who lives here?"

Risa had the grace to blush. "It just seemed like the natural thing to do—strange people, strange environment. I was at a major disadvantage. When I lost my ability to read people, to hear their thoughts, I became isolated, like I was in a vacuum. Knowing what was going on around me made me feel safer. I really didn't mean to intrude, you know, I never watched anything…private. And I'd spent so much time living on government property, and having most things I needed at hand or taken care of, that it's been difficult adjusting. And I had some experience with electronics, so…"

"So wiring into all of our apartments allowed you to

keep track of us so, for instance, you knew I was heading out to the store when you called me to pick up groceries for you," Kristy deduced, frowning slightly.

Risa nodded, feeling distinctly ashamed.

"Yes, I'm sorry for that, too. I'm just not equipped for—" she looked around, waving her arms and letting her frustration show "—this. Everything. The world."

It felt so good to finally talk to someone. Risa had never really had a female friend before. Or a male friend, for that matter. After her parents died, she'd confided her secrets and fears only to Buddy. So far, Kristy was taking what Risa told her in relative stride.

"I could help, you know."

"You have helped, getting my groceries, listening. But you don't have to do that anymore. I wouldn't ask that of you."

"What I mean is I can help you get back into normal life. You know, for instance…" Kristy assessed Risa closely, making her feel like squirming in her chair. "Are those black pants and shirts all you have to wear?"

Risa looked down at her clothes, the government-issued casuals she'd always worn.

"Yes. They're all I need."

"Oh, honey, with your figure you can carry the cat burglar look off nicely, but with your coloring and that amazing auburn hair and those blue eyes—you should be wearing something much more striking."

Kristy's mental makeover was setting Risa's nerves on edge. She wasn't sure she was ready for this, and Kristy had a definite gleam in her eye. Risa didn't need her former powers to sense that her new friend was getting very excited about influencing Risa's life.

"And you have no good furniture, nothing on your walls. The place is stark. No personality. We have to get more of your style in here—what do you like?"

"What do you mean?" Risa could only stare.

"You know, what are your favorite colors, for a start?"

Risa paused for a long moment. She'd never really been asked that before. She thought about Buddy, the rich chocolate-brown of his fur, and remembered the scarlet sweater her mother had been wearing the day she'd brought Buddy home. Her mother had always worn bright colors—why hadn't Risa remembered that until now?

"I like brown. And red."

Kristy pursed her lips thoughtfully. "Well, I've always been more of a pink and yellow girl myself, but we can work with that—earthy tones, I guess. Like clays and fire. Yes, that does seem right for you." She looked at the clock, "Hey, I'll tell you what. I have the day off, why don't we go catch some lunch and hit the stores? It'll be fun."

"Hit the stores?" Risa wasn't quite keeping up, still wondering how all of this had happened.

"Yeppers. C'mon, ex-spy lady. We're going shopping."

2

DANIEL WATCHED Risa from a discreet distance, following the actions of the two women closely. Even though he'd spent thousands of hours doing surveillance, watching Risa felt different. More intimate. Maybe because each new outfit she tried on distracted him from his purpose, among other things. It wasn't as if she were trying on anything particularly sexy, no low-cut dresses or skintight bodysuits—like the ones he'd seen her wearing on missions—clinging to every curve. He couldn't take his eyes off of her, and his interest wasn't completely professional.

He swallowed deeply, trying to ignore the way his pulse picked up when she stepped out of the dressing room, looking to her friend for reassurance that the low-rise jeans and raspberry T-shirt fit.

Oh, man, did they ever fit. The woman had an ass like two perfect scoops of ice cream.

The shirt exposed a delicious sliver of her flat, toned belly, and the stylishly faded denim hugged the gentle sway of her backside in a way that had him imagining cupping his hand over the pocket.

Her friend nodded enthusiastically, obviously having

good taste. Risa received the approval awkwardly, stuffing her hands in the pockets of the jeans, looking furtively from side to side as if worried about being seen. Was she self-conscious or was she worried?

Daniel turned his attention to her shopping partner. His quick background check identified Risa's friend as Kristy Louise Kelly, twenty-five, a Boston native, MIT grad and an oceanographic intern at Woods Hole. He'd seen them sitting at Risa's utilitarian kitchen table that morning, talking over a breakfast that neither one of them touched—but talking about what?

He hadn't had an opportunity to bug the apartment— Risa was *always* there. This was the first time he'd seen her leave, and opted for following rather than a search. He'd assumed if she were venturing out, it must have been important—he'd never have guessed clothes shopping.

However, it appeared she was doing some surveillance of her own, and if he could get over there, he might be able to link into her system. He could find out what she was up to, who she was watching and why. Jack was right—something was off.

Was she finally adjusting on her own, a late bloomer? Why now, all of a sudden, after months of isolation? Could this new "friend" be a problem, someone else who knew about Risa's secrets, or who wanted to know? Daniel intended to find out.

He'd arrived on the Cape a week ago. The small town of Falmouth was as charming as ever. Daniel booked a room at a small motel a few minutes down the street from Risa's apartment complex, even though the home where he'd grown up was only about an hour up the coast. He needed to be closer to watch her movements, to assess the situation.

Though Jack had mentioned his family, there was no need to stir up those old ghosts. He was here to do a job; he'd do it, and move on, hopefully with no one being the wiser. If Kristy Kelly was a real friend, maybe Risa wouldn't need him to interfere in her life, so he could report back to Jack and be assigned something more critical than watching Risa shop.

"Daniel? Oh my God...it *is* you. What are you doing here?"

Daniel turned toward the disbelieving female voice that drew his attention away from Risa and Kristy. Instincts developed after years in the field compelled him to relax, to act naturally so as not to draw attention, even though he simultaneously felt the urge to duck behind the rack of women's lingerie that he'd been standing beside.

When he turned, he looked into eyes as gray as his, set in a female face that also resembled his own. He took in her softer features, his eyes widening as he sighted his younger sister's extremely pregnant belly.

"Anna." He breathed out the name softly, hardly believing she was standing right in front of him. The last time he'd seen her was in New York City just two years ago, where she'd been vacationing and they'd met for dinner. He'd given her a secure e-mail address where she could contact him. He just couldn't break all contact with his youngest sister.

He'd attended her wedding shortly after, staying in the background, and leaving a gift before anyone else knew he was there. His appearance would have caused too much of a scuffle, and it was her day. He hadn't wanted to ruin it, though he'd caught her for one moment before he left. She'd been such a tomboy, keeping up with her brothers effortlessly all those years—and now she was a grown woman. He didn't know she was expecting, though. The discovery threw him. She was his baby sister, and she was having a baby of her own.

"Seven months and counting," she said as if she'd read his mind, her voice as natural as if she met him in the store every day, as if it weren't unusual at all. "I guess that's obvious, though, isn't it? You're going to be an uncle, Daniel."

An uncle. The words rang in his ears like she was speaking to him in a foreign language. He wasn't sure what to say—he'd been a stranger, living a life so apart from them for so long, he wasn't sure he had a right to the title of uncle, or brother or son, for that matter. Not anymore. He noticed the tension that creased her brow as she flipped through a few flimsy robes, not really seeing them. The surprise of finding him here, and the many questions about why he was here, must be finally hitting its mark.

"I wish you'd let me know. I've been out of the country, but I try to check my e-mail," he said.

"It's not the kind of thing you tell someone by e-mail—I would like you to have been here, though."

"I was out of the country for the last year—I left shortly after the last time we spoke."

He ignored the disapproval evident in her expression. She didn't agree with what he did for a living; Anna was a peace-loving creature who shared her family's liberal political views. Those views wouldn't allow them to understand many of the things Daniel did for a living.

"So what are you doing here, Daniel? Have you finally decided to come home and make peace with your demons?"

Daniel felt somehow exposed by his sister's simple inquiry. He also had no idea what was happening with Risa and her friend. He was losing track, was off balance—never a good situation for a field agent.

"I can see I've caught you off guard."

He started to say something—anything—when he caught movement out of the corner of his eye. Two security guards were moving past them, a sense of purpose in their walk. The hairs on the back of Daniel's neck stood up as his instincts kicked into gear. The two men made a beeline for the women's dressing rooms, where Risa and Kristy had been trying on clothes.

"Daniel? What is it?"

"A moment, Anna…"

His focus returned with hawklike clarity as he watched the officers approach the very dressing room where Risa was. They spoke briefly to Kristy, who'd been lounging in a chair by the entryway, blowing bubbles with her gum—she didn't match the image of a oceanographic scientist at all. Though Daniel couldn't hear the conversation, he could see something was wrong. Kristy looked visibly annoyed.

"Daniel, please—"

"Anna, play along with me for the time being, okay?"

"Daniel, I don't know—"

He didn't give her time to complete her objection, grabbing her hand and pulling her along with him as he made his way to the dressing room just in time to see one of the officers gingerly removing Risa from inside by the arm. Her expression was frozen into a mix of surprise, fear and repulsion. He knew he had to get her out of there. The last thing they needed was Risa Remington being taken to the police station.

Risa had been given a fake background documents recording fictional previous addresses, jobs, education and the like. The government had sent her on her way with a credit rating, a bank account and a few credit cards to get her going. She had a Massachusetts driver's license and a car that she didn't appear to use.

If the police checked her out, nothing would seem unusual, but Daniel doubted that she would be able to get through a police interview without drawing more attention to herself than she should. Depending on what she was involved in, if anything, drawing police attention could be dangerous. To her, to him, to anyone involved.

"Help? With what?" Anna huffed slightly as she matched his quick pace and he slowed, but only slightly.

"I'll explain everything later."

Anna grumbled something unintelligible but fell into

step beside him. She would have made a solid agent, if she'd been inclined. She was the sibling he was the closest to; Daniel was one of five, two brothers, two sisters. Anna had always been the earth-mother type; even though she was the youngest, she'd wanted to take care of everyone. He slanted a look at her again, the roses blooming in her cheeks indicating that impending motherhood agreed with her.

The guard was gripping a resistant Risa by the forearm while the other argued with Kristy, who appeared slightly panicked while she tried to reason with the guy. Daniel and Anna cut into the fray.

"Excuse me, is there a problem here?"

All four people spun as he became the center of attention, and he saw the surprise reflected in Risa's face as her eyes met his—as well as apprehension, and suspicion.

"What are you doing here?" Her tone was far from welcoming, and he ignored the daggers she shot in his direction.

"Officers, is there a problem?"

"Yeah. Who are you?"

He slipped his arm around Anna and sighed, smiling at Risa indulgently. He hoped she would see that he was here to help her and not spit in his face, like it looked as if she were ready to do.

"My name is Daniel MacAlister. This is my sister Anna. Our family lives in Harwich. And this—" he stared at Risa with all the appearance of affection that he could muster "—is my fiancée, Risa Remington.

Now, if you would you take your hands off of her, please, and tell me what's going on?"

"FIANCÉE?" Risa looked on, just as shocked as anyone. Anna and Kristy spoke in unison, shock evident in their voices, as Agent MacAlister's eyes held hers. Risa's voice clogged in her throat as she tried to protest, but all that came out was a strangled sound that didn't even resemble words. MacAlister was putting on quite a show—he looked positively doting. But she read the warning behind his false affection clearly: *go along, don't make a fuss.*

She was in a jam, no doubt. But to pretend she was his fiancée? How had he managed to pop up at just this exact moment? How long had he been watching her, and who had sent him? Why was he here? She had more questions, but she knew she wouldn't get any answers to them in a jail cell. Having Secret Agent Daniel MacAlister pop up in your life was not a good thing, in Risa's experience.

"Fiancée, huh?" The guard turned to stare at MacAlister. "She doesn't sound all that pleased to see you."

"She's just annoyed, and I can't say I blame her."

Risa had been pissed to discover the camera in the dressing room—she didn't like being watched—and was even angrier now that she saw who sat on the other end of the lens. She was more than capable of voicing her objections about such treatment, but no one was listening to her.

No one would have dared to ignore her if she still had her powers. She knew ordinary women were dismissed and discriminated against in society all the time, but she hadn't been an ordinary woman. People had always listened to what she had to say. Some had feared her, but at the very least, she'd commanded respect.

She wasn't commanding anything at the moment. The frustration—the overwhelming feeling of being horribly, helplessly normal—assaulted her as the three men discussed her situation as if she weren't even there.

"Well, your fiancée crawled up through the ceiling panel and disconnected the surveillance cameras. We had no choice but to suspect she and her friend were trying to make off with stolen purchases."

"My fiancée has no need to steal. I can provide her with whatever she needs."

Risa nearly had a stroke on the spot, so furious she couldn't speak.

"Why else would she shut the cameras off? Either way, she was caught tampering with store property, and—"

"Excuse me." Risa's voice was an acid drip into the conversation, and everyone became quiet. MacAlister's eyes shuttered and she could see the tension that drew his features tight—he didn't like it that she'd interfered. Well, too bad.

"You—" she glared at the man holding her arm "—have no right to be watching women while they are changing their clothes. You're lucky I didn't take that camera and cram it up—"

Daniel interrupted, laughing loudly enough to interrupt the end of her sentence. "Sweetheart, no need to sink to their level."

She turned her glare on him, disliking intensely how he insinuated himself between her and the guard who held her arm, breaking the connection to replace it with his own as he wrapped his arm around her shoulders. She almost pulled away, but the pressure of his fingers warned her not to. The store's manager had joined them, coming down the aisle at a near run, breathless when he arrived.

Daniel spoke loudly enough to make sure the manager heard him clearly amid the din, inserting just the right amount of male outrage into his tone.

"She's absolutely right. Aren't there laws about that kind of thing? I think the local papers would be interested in what's happened here, and I can't imagine the damage that would be done when the story comes out. Take her down to your offices, and I'll contact the media about this matter right away."

Anna, the woman whom MacAlister had identified as his sister, popped in and said, "Yes, absolutely. I shop here all the time, and I don't want anyone watching me dress in dressing rooms. It's despicable!"

Risa had no idea why MacAlister was here, why his sister was defending her or why no one seemed to think she could fight her own battles, but she didn't need super powers to know he wanted her to stay quiet. The manager was turning increasingly pale as Risa felt her own face redden.

"Now, sir, Mr....?"

"MacAlister. Daniel MacAlister."

"Mr. MacAlister, I can assure you we always have a female employee review those tapes, and the only reason security was called was because your fiancée was last recorded disconnecting the cameras."

"She's shy."

"Yes, well, um, of course, but we are within our legal rights to monitor for shoplifting."

Daniel's voice turned cool. "You won't have to worry about shoplifting after we tell every woman on the Cape that you watch them change their clothes—and tape it."

The man stuttered, obviously rethinking his decision, and blinked quickly, trying to backpedal. "Now, I don't think we need to let this little incident get out of hand. I'm sure your fiancée didn't mean any harm, and we appreciate your business. Would you like me to take your purchases to the counter?"

Daniel looked at Risa, their eyes meeting in a clash of blue and gray. She was easily six inches shorter than his solid five-ten. Standing so close, he could detect the clean scent of soap and shampoo, and found himself staring. She wore no makeup; she didn't need it. She was flawless, her burnished locks warming porcelain skin, decorated by a playful spray of freckles over her nose. He'd never noticed those before. Why was he noticing now?

And why was he so acutely aware of how close they were standing, and of how curvy she was? His voice was hoarse when he spoke, and he cleared his throat, telling himself his behavior would be exactly what would be expected from a lover. He was just acting convincingly for the benefit of their onlookers.

"I don't know. What do you think, sweetheart? You've been through a terrible embarrassment here. First the indignity of the cameras, and then being manhandled—"

"Twenty-five percent off everything you're buying," the manager interjected quickly, looking at them with dire hope the entire matter could be averted. Other customers had started paying attention.

Daniel could see that Risa's temper hadn't cooled down, but the sooner he could get her out of here, the better. Kristy, thankfully, spoke up.

"Make it forty and we're outta here."

"Forty it is."

"Dammit, I don't care about—" Risa was spitting mad, and wasn't about to be bought off, especially with clothes. But before she could finish her sentence, Daniel loomed in close and kissed her.

She hadn't seen it coming—she wouldn't have seen it coming in a million years, not in her wildest imagination. She hadn't been kissed since her parents died, and never by a man. Certainly never like *this*.

Shock and curiosity mingled as MacAlister's mouth touched hers, stopping her words and confusing her thoughts. It was a strange feeling, and it captured her total attention as she forgot where they were and what was going on around them. Nothing else mattered except for the feeling of warmth she experienced, the soft press of his lips to hers. She shuffled closer, seeking more until someone cleared their throat.

Risa was in a daze when MacAlister drew back, looking just as composed as he always did. He hadn't been affected at all. The corner of the very perfect lips that had just met hers quirked up, and something heated inside her. She felt like hitting him—hard—but she also felt like kissing him again. She couldn't take her eyes off of his mouth.

When she realized that he no longer held her, and that both of her hands had somehow found their way to his shoulders and lingered there, she stepped back, turning away. Her pin-straight hair fell forward around her face, hiding her from the onlookers as MacAlister settled the situation with the manager. Risa wanted to hide, to process what had happened and to get away from the crowd. The urge to run, to get back to her apartment where she was safe, assailed her.

What were all these people thinking? She dared to look up, finding the manager looking relieved as MacAlister spoke to him quietly. Anna, MacAlister's sister, was studying Risa curiously, sending Risa back into hiding behind her hair. Kristy was gathering up the clothes she'd tried on, triumphant in wrangling a discount. Risa looked down, her fingers touching the small white tag hanging from the T-shirt she had on.

Kristy touched her hand and Risa drew back reflexively, as she always did. Except with MacAlister. Her fingers moved to her lips as she remembered the kiss—it was a touch, an intimate one, and she hadn't drawn back. She'd stepped closer. There hadn't been any painful blankness or sense of disconnection. In fact, MacAlister's kiss was the first time she'd felt connected to something, to someone, since she'd awakened from her coma. Realizing it made her want to run—and made her want to have more.

She was staring at him, and he pursed his warm lips thoughtfully, staring right back as if he had every right to look at her so possessively.

"C'mon, you two. Enough of the lovey-dovey stuff." Kristy broke the visual lock between them, handing Risa some purchases to carry as she leaned in close, whispering, "And you have some explaining to do—fiancé, huh?"

MacAlister must have overheard, and when Risa opened her mouth to correct Kristy, she closed it again, thinking better of it. She didn't know why MacAlister was here.

She smiled at Kristy. "It was a surprise. It's not what you think."

"Yeah, there seems to be a lot of that with you." She winked. "What a hottie. I wouldn't mind having a surprise like that. Maybe two."

Risa was thankful that her new friend appeared to be teasing, and Risa dutifully followed her to the counter, where they could pay and get out.

Risa wondered what the agency had deemed so important they'd send one of their top field operatives. Daniel MacAlister was no lightweight—she'd worked with him before and she'd rarely met anyone so focused on his work, so determined to get the job done. He was intelligent, dedicated and lethal. Apparently, this time, his mission involved her.

If he'd come to kill her, she'd be dead already. A

man like that wouldn't bother wasting his time dallying in department stores; he could have picked her off cleanly, no matter where she was. She also knew, while MacAlister had killed in the line of duty, he wasn't an assassin. So it had to be something else.

Hope sparked suddenly as her mind worked over the scenarios—maybe the agency had changed their position on her employment and had a use for her even if she didn't have her superpowers. Could he have been sent to retrieve her for service?

"God, he's incredible! Look at that butt…." Kristy sighed as she shamelessly ogled Daniel, who walked just ahead of them. Risa wondered if he'd heard; if so, he gave no indication. He *was* handsome, she thought rather experimentally; she wasn't used to thinking about men in those terms. The only men she'd been around were Dr. Laslow and the operatives she'd worked with—or the terrorists and other subjects she'd had to examine. Needless to say, she'd never noticed any of their backsides. She tried not to notice MacAlister's, but Kristy was right—it was nicely shaped. Toned, tapered, muscular. She felt her pulse pick up a little, and looked away, focusing on Anna, who walked at his side.

Risa was dying to get out of the store and get some answers. The security guards and manager were gone, crisis averted. As the clerk rang up her purchases while Kristy watched to make sure she received her forty percent discount, Risa moved closer to where MacAlister stood, silent and watchful.

"I'm not your fiancée."

He shifted cool eyes to meet hers, and arched an eyebrow, shaking his head ever so slightly as if to say *not now.* How could she read him so clearly, without so much as a word spoken between them? The connection she had with him drew her, in spite of her worries about his presence.

"I don't believe that's your sister. Is she another agent—"

"I most certainly am not," Anna interrupted. "I am his sister, one of two. Apparently, Daniel hasn't told you much about the family he's trying to convince you to join."

Anna had rejoined them after breaking away to pay for her own purchases, and MacAlister's very nice lips thinned as he realized his sister had overheard Risa.

Anna turned to Daniel. "Is this why you've come back to the Cape, Daniel? To tell us you're getting married?"

MacAlister—Daniel—looked like a cat about to crawl right out of his skin. Risa crossed her arms and gave him the same cool look he'd been sending her. It was his story that they were engaged, let him deal with the fallout.

"Not exactly. That was a small lie, I have to confess."

"Why am I not surprised?" Anna sounded dismally disappointed.

"Risa and I were in a…relationship. She quit and moved away, and we never had the chance to really share our feelings. Work was always in the way. I came here to remedy that."

Risa turned, thinking she heard the sales clerk sigh— or was it Kristy? Still, she said nothing, holding his gaze in a dare. The next thing she knew, Anna was at her side, sliding her arm through Risa's and hugging her close. Risa stiffened at the contact, ready to bolt, but Anna's hold was firm.

The expectant mother shined at Risa, then at her brother. The reality sank in for Risa—they really were brother and sister. Anna was not an undercover operative working with Daniel, or some woman he'd randomly picked up in the store for cover. Everything took on a surreal blur that Risa couldn't process.

Anna's voice was joyful as she said, "Well, I don't care what the reason is. The important thing is that you're back, and if Risa is the reason for that, then we'll all welcome her with open arms. She's part of the family already, as far as I'm concerned."

For the first time since this entire fiasco began, Risa saw uncertainty flicker in Agent MacAlister's placid gray eyes. Smiling brightly in his direction, she capitalized on the weakness she'd found and hugged Anna's arm closer.

"Well, *Daniel*," she said his name deliberately, getting used to the less formal address, "I'm very interested in anything you came here to tell me."

3

"CAN I ASK YOU something?"

Kristy's voice interrupted Risa's thoughts, scattered as they were. All she wanted to do was get back to her apartment and find out what the hell Daniel MacAlister was up to. He claimed that Risa was the reason he was staying in Falmouth instead of with his family in Harwich, but that was just a cover. Risa knew he had to be on assignment, and she needed details. She responded to Kristy absently, hoping there wasn't going to be more talk about how attractive Daniel was.

"Sure, what?"

"Do you watch *everyone* in the building?"

"I'll disconnect the monitors. I told you why I did it. I know it was wrong, but—"

"No, I don't mean it that way. I just wondered. How did you do it? It's sort of creepy, you know, in general. Someone can be watching you at any time, even in your own home, and you have no idea."

She shuddered, and Risa felt terrible—guilt was an emotion that had been largely regarded as useless in her life. She couldn't do her work if she was going to feel guilty about prying into people's thoughts, etc. But it was different this time—most of the people she'd scanned before were terrorists, enemies, but Kristy was neither.

"I was good with technology when I worked for the government."

She thought back to all the hours, days and weeks when she'd been glued to computer networks, sifting through a constant barrage of information, trying to catch any stray byte that would be meaningful to the analysts at the Pentagon. It was a more intense connection, more difficult to maintain, than reading people, and once she'd gotten inside of the stream of information, it was often difficult getting back out. She'd shorted out like an overloaded circuit several times before they figured out how much she could take. Even then, Dr. Laslow had pressed her limits, always reminding her how important her work was. After her parents' deaths, her work became her purpose, the thing she held on to that was constant in her life. If she ever felt lonely, she'd learned to push it aside.

It was an added benefit that all the residual knowledge, all of her understanding of how computers and networks worked, had stayed with her. She knew computers as well as she knew her own heartbeat. This wasn't something she could share with Kristy, obviously. For her friend's safety, the less she knew, the better.

However, Risa had never really had any conflict about her work or about spying on the people in her apartment building. She'd been taught to do what was necessary, and that's what she'd done. She herself was exposed and studied in every aspect of her life, by

Laslow and the government; it was the norm for her. But Kristy reminded her that most people expected privacy.

"It's not difficult to get basic surveillance equipment if you know where to look, and since the building already had a decent security system, I just worked with that and added some enhancements. Mostly at night, or when people were out at work, gone shopping, stuff like that."

"Even Ben Richter, on the third floor?"

Risa turned her head, detecting a subtle change in Kristy's tone—why was she asking these questions?

"Yeah, even him. Why?"

"I've been crazy about him for months, but he doesn't even know I'm alive. He works at the same lab I do. He's here for a year from Germany as part of Ridge 2000— the program studying the midocean ridges. I thought he was just shy, but I can't seem to strike up a conversation, or anything," she confessed hurriedly.

"Maybe he's not into women."

Kristy smiled, though Risa didn't understand what was so funny. It was a logical deduction that if a man wasn't interested in an attractive woman like Kristy, then one of the reasons could be that he was gay. Or married. Or both.

"Nah, thanks for the vote of confidence, but I don't think I'm that irresistible. And I've seen him out with girls. Believe me, those looks combined with his accent—Oh, my God, just hearing him say 'good morning' turns my knees to water—any red-blooded woman within hearing distance is toast. I never would have thought a German accent would be sexy, but oh, my."

"That doesn't mean he's not gay."

"How do you figure?"

"I read the minds of many men who had homoerotic tendencies, most of them buried in the subconscious. They didn't even realize it themselves. Most of them were married or actively hetero. A lot of people simply can't deal with those repressed feelings."

Kristy shrugged. "I guess it's possible. But I just have a gut feeling it's not true in Ben's case."

Risa turned, interested. "Gut feeling?"

"Yeah, you know, an instinct. You just kind of know when something is true, even when all signs would indicate otherwise. Intuition, I guess. You know what I mean?"

"No, not really." Risa scowled and looked out the window—she had sensed some things about people around her, Kristy and Daniel, but she found the vague indications of moods or tones aggravating after spending a lifetime accessing specific information. "I thought you were more of a scientific type?"

"I am. I am a solid supporter of the scientific method. However, the really big advances, the breakthroughs in science, are usually based on intuition. Those inklings can lead a scientist in the right direction."

"If you say so."

Kristy shot her a disbelieving look. "Don't you get 'gut feelings'?"

Risa wasn't sure how to answer. "Dr. Laslow said my instincts weren't as developed as normal people's since I could simply find out what I needed to know with a touch. My superior strength meant I didn't have the strong fight-or-flight responses that normal people have. Now I can sense some things about people or situations, but it's not something I trust—I don't know how anyone could trust it."

Kristy passed over that idea to hone in on what Risa had let slip. "You were superstrong, too? Is that part of the psychic thing?"

Risa cursed herself silently—she had to be more careful. "I'd been working for the government, and in physical training, pretty much since I was born. I guess I was just in better physical shape from childhood than most people," she hedged.

Of course, that wouldn't explain why she didn't have that same strength now, and she hoped her shrewd friend didn't ask. Risa spoke quickly, filling the gap before Kristy could inquire anymore deeply.

"I've always been curious about things like intuition and gut feelings, though. When you have a feeling about something, do you actually feel it? Is it sensation? Pain?"

"No, not actual pain. I don't know if it's the same for everyone, but I get a kind of sinking feeling in my stomach if I think something bad is happening. Or, for instance, every time I see Ben, I just *know* that if I could get his attention, we'd be great together."

"And you trust these feelings? Without knowing for sure?"

"Completely."

Risa thought about the warm, pleasant sensation she'd had when MacAlister had kissed her, but she wasn't comfortable discussing it. She'd assumed everyone had that reaction to being kissed, but maybe it came down to chemistry? What did that mean for her and MacAlister? Was that the same kind of gut feeling Kristy had for Ben?

"But Ben's never talked to you? You don't know him?"

"Not much. Basic conversation, hello, goodbye, how are you? That's it. But I can't get my mind off of him. Anyway, I was thinking if I had an inside line, if I knew about his interests, or what he does outside of work, you know, like where he was going this Saturday, then maybe I might fare a little better."

"You want me to spy on Ben so you can try to seduce him." This made sense, and Risa smiled. So maybe Kristy's gut feelings weren't so sure—she wanted something more solid to go on.

Kristy smiled, pulling onto Falmouth's main street, heading toward their apartment building. "I guess that's the direct way of putting it. I don't want to really spy on him, I just thought…"

"You don't want me disconnecting my monitors?"

Risa was surprised—and a little worried. Should she do this for Kristy? She tried to quiet her mind and listen to her "gut feelings" but she couldn't—her rational mind took over. What Kristy was asking was harmless, as long as they kept it under control.

"Sure, we can see what he's up to this weekend," Risa agreed. "But I don't watch anything too private, so no looking when he's walking around naked."

"He walks around the apartment n-naked?" Kristy's mouth dropped open, and Risa smiled, saying nothing. This could be fun.

DANIEL WATCHED the two women a few car lengths ahead of him as they raced back up Route 6 toward Falmouth. They appeared to be talking animatedly, and he wondered about what. His mission had been accelerated whether he liked it or not.

Having family on the Cape gave him a good cover— but he hadn't counted on bumping into Anna. He gripped the wheel more tightly, barely noticing the landscape around him while he drove. The area hadn't changed too much over the years—more stores, more people, but it was still relatively deserted. The swell of tourist season was a few months away.

Keeping an eye on Risa would have been easier with more people around—he could get lost in the crowd. Instead, his sister had found him lurking in the women's lingerie department at the mall, where he'd stood out like a sore thumb. He'd come up with a believable explanation off the cuff, but now he had more problems. Anna knew he was here, and the rest of his family would know before long.

Although he'd managed to back out of the fiancé story, there remained several kinks in his cover. He needed to have a convincing reason he wasn't staying in Harwich, at his family's home. Pursuing a love interest in Falmouth was the first option that had popped into his mind.

Risa wasn't buying any of it, of course. He had to

spin the story differently to reassure her that she was safe, and not send her running—especially if she was up to something. Partial truths always worked better than outright lies; he could admit to checking up on her, making sure she was adjusting, but also claim to be visiting his family.

Would she believe that he'd been harboring a latent attraction to her all those years, and had come to try to make good on it now? Maybe capitalizing on pulling her out of the lab, saving her life? Possible, though he was less comfortable with that angle. Playing both ends of his story was tricky, but not impossible; he'd certainly been in tougher situations. This was merely inconvenient.

While he'd had his share of affairs, he couldn't afford to think about Risa that way, not until he knew what was going on. He never let himself get involved that way on the job unless it was unavoidable—and only if he could retain complete control of the situation. Something told him that would not be the case with Risa.

However, he couldn't quite erase the lingering sensation of their kiss. He had no idea what had compelled him to kiss Risa. In spite of himself, he'd been carried away, just for a second, shocked at her softness, stunned at his own pulsing reaction to her. Remembering the moment had his heart rate spiking disconcertingly.

Risa wasn't experienced, he knew that, but the way she'd leaned in had a sweetness he hadn't anticipated. She'd responded with more curiosity than desire, but he'd found it just as inflaming. She was beautiful. Innocent—at least in the physical sense. How could a young woman have a normal sex life with Risa's powers? Not to mention growing up in a government lab where she was constantly monitored.

As they pulled into the small parking lot in front of her apartment building, he slowed down, lengthening the distance between them, and instead of following, he took a sharp right and hit the gas. He had to think, to process what had happened. Now wasn't the time to confront her. She'd want answers, explanations, and he had to think, to get the upper hand. Whatever happened between them would be on his terms, not hers.

"Okay, fess up."

Kristy cornered her as soon as they got through the apartment door, lugging all of the bags that they'd brought home from the store. God, how many clothes did Kristy think she needed? Risa was only one woman, and she'd done well wearing more or less the same outfits for twenty-six years. What was she going to do with all of this stuff?

Hoping to deflect the conversation she knew was looming, Risa bent and picked up a scrap of leopard-print silk that slipped from one of the bags.

"What's this?"

"That, sweetie, is a thong. Fashion's brilliant way of avoiding pantylines."

Risa held it up, investigating the thin string of fabric that she logically realized would go… Her gaze swerved back to Kristy. "No way am I wearing this."

"You'll have to at least try it—amazingly comfortable. Men love them—very sexy—so stop stalling. I told you about my crush, so now you tell me about yours."

"There's not much to tell."

She had no idea why Daniel MacAlister was here. Why had he intruded and gotten her out of trouble? Kissed her? And then disappeared? Kristy seemed to see Daniel's appearance as romantic. She wouldn't if she knew him, and what he was capable of.

"Um, guys don't usually materialize out of nowhere, save the day, proclaim they have feelings for you, oh, yeah, and kiss the daylights out of you in front of anyone who's watching. Share."

Risa sighed, relenting. "I did work with him, and it was strictly professional. If he had feelings, I never knew, and I don't want to."

Kristy's eyes widened with concern. "I'm picking up a weird vibe from you—is he stalking you?"

"No, no. Nothing like that." Risa dismissed the idea with a frown. "I don't know what he's up to."

"Risa, if he's not a danger, a man like that is not to be cast aside lightly. Did you see those eyes? He was looking at you like he could have eaten you in one big bite."

"He probably could," she murmured to herself, not wanting to pursue this conversation anymore. To redirect Kristy, she flicked on the monitor and switched the feed to Ben's room, relieved when she saw her upstairs neighbor's image fill the screen. Kristy was immediately distracted.

"He's soooo cute, I can't stand it. Look at his furniture! I knew he'd have good taste. I could tell by the way he dressed, even though I usually see him with his lab coat on. Oh, my…and he's flexible, too."

Kristy and Risa observed Ben on the computer monitor, moving through his stretches before he started performing a set of powerful martial arts moves, battling an invisible assailant. Risa recognized the expertise in his abilities, the smoothness of his movements, the concentration on his face. Ben didn't move like an amateur. Still, a lot of people studied martial arts. There were three schools in the local area.

"My guess is that he holds at least one black belt. I had a few lessons myself—and Ben looks pretty advanced."

Kristy made a fanning motion in front of her face, even though it was a cool sixty-three degrees in the apartment. "God, that makes him even hotter. He's like James Bond or something behind his geeky lab coat. Does he really walk around naked? Or were you just yanking me?"

Risa rolled her eyes.

"C'mon, tell me."

"I only saw him do it once. I don't watch him often because he…"

"Wasn't going to grocery shop for you?"

Risa nodded, her cheeks staining.

"What else can you tell me about him?"

"Like what?"

"C'mon—if you saw him naked, even once, you've seen the goods, right? Impressive? Average? Museum-worthy or garage sale?"

Risa crunched her eyebrows again, unsure exactly what Kristy was hinting at.

Kristy sighed exaggeratedly. "How *big* is he? You know, down *there?*"

Risa's eyes went wide with realization, and she suddenly couldn't resist teasing. She marveled at it for a moment—she hadn't felt this sensation in, well, as long as she could recall. She smiled, shrugging.

"It's hard to tell—everything looks small on the screen."

Kristy moaned in frustration, and then laughed, continuing to watch Ben work out. Ben Richter was attractive, she supposed. Risa knew about sex—in the technical sense. With her powers, Dr. Laslow wouldn't permit anyone to come that close to her, and her life wasn't one that encouraged relationships to blossom. She thought about sex from time to time out of natural curiosity, but it was such a nonissue in her life that she'd gotten used to putting it out of her mind.

However, if she were completely truthful, she'd admit that she had noticed Daniel MacAlister more than once—he was difficult to ignore. There was something about him that had always grabbed her attention. He stood apart, though she'd never really thought about why.

She'd been on a team with him for the first time when she was only eighteen. She remembered feeling awkward in his presence, something that hadn't ever happened before. There'd been one point on the mission when he'd stripped down to change into a diving suit, and she'd had to curl her fingers into her palms to stop from running a hand down his chest. She hadn't understood the urge—it had shocked her on some basic level.

She knew the power of her touch meant it was forbidden for her to lay hands on anyone she worked with. It was standard operating procedure, and she'd never been tempted to break the rules. Until she'd seen *him*.

When they'd returned, Dr. Laslow hadn't been happy with her biofeedback, which had clued him in to how distracted she'd been, and why. A long lecture on her duties, on maintaining focus, had resulted. Risa had worked hard not to let it happen again. Natural curiosity or not, her work was too important to let silly things like sex interfere.

That wasn't the case now. However, as fascinated as she was by her response to MacAlister's kiss, she doubted it was going to happen again.

"Oh, here we go—a phone call. Maybe this will tell me something interesting."

Risa's attention swung back to the screen. Ben picked up the phone and Kristy pumped up the volume until his voice could be heard clearly.

"Oh, he's going to meet friends out—male friends by the sound of it. No trace of a girlfriend waiting in the wings so far."

"Do you know the place he mentioned?"

"I do. And he's going to be there at seven, so I think I might just be there, too."

"Sounds like you have a good plan."

Kristy bit her lip. "But it would look bad for me to just be standing around in a bar, like I do that all the time, you know, hanging out and picking up guys."

"That's bad?"

Kristy rolled her eyes. "Yes, unless you only want a one-night pickup, and I'm hoping for a little more than that with Ben. Maybe a lot more."

"How can you know?"

"I told you—I have a feeling."

"Right. The feeling."

It was all very complicated, and Risa suspected she was fortunate to have skipped this part of human relationships.

"You have to come with me. You can wear that new dress we bought."

Risa stepped back, hands up. "No. No way."

"You don't do alcohol?"

Risa had never touched a drop—she'd been on a strictly regimented diet at the compound. "I've never had it."

"You've never been to a bar? Never had a beer, even as a teenager? What else haven't you done?"

Risa didn't answer, but felt heat move up into her face. She hated that—it never used to happen, unless she was angry or being chastised—but now it seemed like every five minutes her face was turning red.

Kristy somehow understood and she clapped a hand over her astonished expression. Risa was amazed at the level of communication humans could share without saying anything.

"Oh, honey…*really?*"

Risa answered coolly, hoping to put an end to the conversation. "I appreciate you wanting me to come with you, but I'd really rather stay here. You must have other friends you could go with…."

Kristy shook her head, stepping forward and taking

both of Risa's hands in hers. "I don't—not here. All of the women at work are older or married and with families. My friends are all back in Boston. I know it's a lot for you, but it would be fun for you to get out, to live a little. Sounds like you missed a lot while you were working for the government. Don't you deserve to have some fun? To have a life?"

The words burned through Risa's objections and stoked the flames of deeply hidden desires and curiosities so long denied. While she knew that Kristy was being convincing partly for self-serving reasons, Risa wondered if she wasn't right. She *had* missed out on a lot. If she had to be stuck in this "normal" life, maybe it was time she started grabbing it by the horns and catching up.

She lifted the bags and looked at Kristy, relenting. "You think I should wear the red dress?"

4

DANIEL SAT ON THE EDGE of his bed, flipping through Laslow's reports on Risa—he was supposed to destroy them as per Jack's orders, but he'd held on to the files, reading them again to remind himself that what he was seeing was real. His eyes moved over one paragraph:

> 1992. Mission objective: detect terrorist communications on emerging Internet chatrooms— sift through data to select most likely targets and associations. The resource collapsed after six hours of sifting, emergency care implemented. More effective use of our resource in this capacity will require research to prevent overloads. The resource seems to experience great deal of pain when not protected from overload, though all of its physical indicators show no permanent damage. Increased healing capacity? More experiments need to be done to define its upper and lower ranges of sensitivity.

He'd known that Risa had mind-reading abilities, but no one outside of her handlers really knew the total extent of her powers. Most knowledgeable of all was the author of the reports, Dr. Peter Laslow, who'd been studying and training her since birth. Now Daniel knew everything, too, and he was having difficulty reconciling it all. Little he read in the reports seemed reflective of the woman he'd met in the store today.

He winced every time Laslow referred to Risa as "the resource" or "it." Daniel knew it was to protect her identity should the files get into the wrong hands, but still. She'd been just thirteen years old when that entry was written.

She'd been used for just about everything he could imagine—interrogations, most frequently. When she was barely more than a child she'd spent weeks on end meeting with some of the worst terrorist suspects on the planet, probing their minds for what information she could relay to her handlers.

The notes detailed a string of collapses occurring with increased frequency in the adolescent years. Some were more serious than others as they discovered and tested the limits of her powers. They'd eventually developed ways for her to filter what her mind grabbed on to, to protect herself—not out of compassion, but because they couldn't risk losing her as an asset. After her accident, she'd suffered frequent blackouts and headaches; Daniel wondered if they were still happening.

He'd seen the ravages of terrorism. The images were scarred onto his mind. But Risa had actually been *inside* of the minds of people who committed, or intended to commit, some of the worst crimes in history. She'd learned their languages and had been a part of them when she explored their minds. What did that do to a person? Could she ever adjust to ordinary life?

Hell, he'd had a wonderful, loving childhood. Even in the course of his work, he hadn't been subjected to half of what she had, but he didn't think he could ever go back to ordinary life again. In fact, he knew he couldn't. Once he'd seen the utter destruction one person could wreak upon another, and even more disturbing, what he himself was capable of, there was no way to work back from that.

The thought distracted him—his situation at the moment was difficult. There were eight messages on his room's phone, all from his family. Three were from his mother. Anna hadn't wasted any time getting the word out. They were voices from another lifetime—familiar and foreign all at once, connecting to something deep inside of him he'd thought was gone. But he had no intention of responding, at least not until he knew what was going on with Risa. Just being around his family could put them in danger if Risa were aligning herself with bad people. Daniel would rather risk his family's ire than their safety.

Levering himself up, he grabbed his keys. He was back on task. Rereading the files reaffirmed his mission, reminding him why he was here. Risa could be a threat. She'd also been a victim, the way he saw it, but he had to push that aside and deal with the facts. If she was a problem, he'd have to take care of it.

It was still light outside, but it would be dark soon enough—the long days of summer weren't here yet. The air had a nip in it, though his leather jacket was comfortable. He slid into the car, pulling into traffic and heading toward Risa's apartment complex.

When he got there, he saw Risa getting into a car with Kristy. They were dressed for a night out, Kristy in snug black pants and a tight white top, and Risa in a flirty dress that showed way too much leg as she slipped into the passenger seat. The alarm buzzed in the back of his mind again—she didn't come off as the antisocial woman he'd been sent to watch. He fell in far enough behind that he couldn't be spotted, and followed.

"I DON'T SEE HIM."

Kristy craned her neck, looking all around the Sand Bar, a small local tavern overlooking Cape Cod Bay. The tide was low, and the mud flats stretched out far ahead of them. Some people were walking and a couple of dogs were splashing in puddles of seawater. The picnic tables and outdoor seating were not available; it was early May, but still a little cool in the evenings.

Risa scanned the bar with her. A few patrons had gathered in small groups, talking and sharing plates of greasy-looking food. Risa's beer sat on the table in front of her; she'd tried it, but she didn't care for the bitter taste.

Some more people filed in, and another person set the jukebox to playing. It was fascinating to watch, to feel part of the world, though she knew Kristy was growing worried that Ben wasn't coming. It was almost nine o'clock. Risa tried her hand at comforting Kristy.

"He's probably just late. Maybe he had to pick someone up?"

"I suppose. Let's not list punctuality as one of his virtues, then." Kristy made a valiant effort to turn her attention to Risa and away from the door. "The beer isn't working for you?"

"Not really."

Just then, a waitress came up to them and put two colorful-looking drinks on the table.

"We didn't order these," Kristy objected.

The waitress nodded over to the corner of the bar with a wink. "Those guys sent them over—said you two should have something more colorful."

Kristy looked again, and raised her glass to the guys at the table in a measured motion of thanks, before returning her gaze to the door.

"I wish Ben would get here. We're going to start getting picked up left and right if we're just sitting here alone." She sipped her drink and made an appreciative sound in Risa's direction. "Try this one, it's a daiquiri— you'll find it much better than beer, I think. Might as well enjoy them—mixed drinks are expensive." She grinned, sipping again.

Risa took a tentative sip, and her eyes widened in pleased surprise. "This is good! We should go over and say thank you." She sipped again.

Kristy shook her head and reached across to place her hand over Risa's.

"Wow, you really are out of touch, huh? Listen, those guys are way older than us, and they're only out here looking for one thing."

"What's that?"

"You don't want to know. Smile nicely, but not in the way that invites them over—nod once, then cut eye contact. If they come over, let me handle it."

Risa shrugged, doing as she was told, enjoying the drink. It was more like a dessert, almost. Better, perhaps, than her beloved chocolate pudding.

"Take it easy—that's going to go to your head…oh! There he is—he's here!"

Risa looked up from her drink to see Ben Richter walk into the bar; he was with two other men. They didn't see her or Kristy, and walked in the other direction toward some empty seats at the bar.

"Crap, he'll never see me from way over there…."

"You'll have to arrange a meet," Risa said conspiratorially, frowning when she saw her drink was almost gone. "But don't be obvious. Finish your drink, and then go up to get another one. You can get one for me, too."

She felt great. She couldn't remember being this relaxed, and it was all to the credit of the frothy pink beverage. She wanted another one, but was willing to wait for Kristy to finish hers.

"Are you okay? You look a little flushed."

Risa made a pooh-poohing gesture, waving away her friend's concerns. "I'm fine. Believe me, I know my limist, uh, I mean, limits. They spent years testing them."

Kristy's eyebrows shot up as Risa scanned the bar, continuing. "I have a better idea. Let me go get the drinks. It will probably be smoother if I run interference—I'm not interested in him. If you ho, I mean, if you go, he may pick up on something."

"You think?"

"Absolutely. Believe me, I'm a professional. I've done things like this a million times before."

Kristy looked doubtful, but sat back in her chair.

"Okay. But ask the bartender for your drink to be virgin this time—you don't need two of these. Trust me. Just get me a Diet Coke. I'm driving, so no more alcohol for me. In fact, order some wings while you're there."

Risa's grin was irrepressible. "Virgin. Ha. And wings. Okay."

Risa casually inserted herself in an open space at the bar where Ben sat. When the bartender took her order, she decided against Kristy's advice and just handed the guy her almost empty glass.

"Two more of those. And some wings, please."

"Hot buffalo, Mexican-lime or honey-garlic?"

"What? Wings. We want some *wings,* please." She'd read in a book that service people were often treated rudely, and she made a point to keep her voice polite, but maybe some of that rudeness came from people having to repeat themselves, she figured. The bartender waited, pen in hand.

"I think he wants to know what kind," Ben Richter interrupted, amused. Risa turned, smiling at him.

"Oh. I never ordered wings before. The Mexican-lines—lime—ones, please."

Ben stared at her for a long moment. "Don't I know you?"

"No. Not really. I mean, I live downstairs from you."

Realization dawned on his face. "Yes! Of course. I didn't recognize you...you look different."

"It's the dress." She took a little sip of her drink as he looked up and down once, appreciatively.

"A very nice dress, indeed. Are you here alone?"

"Oh, no. My friend Kristy is out with me. She's helping me get a life."

Ben's brow furrowed before he laughed and looked to where she'd indicated Kristy, smiling in recognition, sitting at the table.

"I work with her."

"Really? You should come join us. Kristy's great," she added, feeling like the best new friend in the world. "I'm going back to our table, but come by and say hello."

"Will do, beautiful."

Risa smiled, and took a step, stopping to blink and catch her balance. Ben took her elbow.

"Careful there. Let me help you."

"Thanks."

Risa couldn't believe how easy this was—she was doing great. Ben walked with her back to the table, where she smiled triumphantly at Kristy. Mission accomplished.

"Kristy, I think you know Ben—he said he works with you?" She sat and smiled at them, pleased with her matchmaking success.

"Hi, Ben—it's a small world. We live in the same place, work in the same place, and now here we are, in the same place." Kristy's smile was flirty, and Ben smiled back.

"I don't want to interrupt your party, but I think our neighbor is a little tipsy."

Risa had already emptied half of the second lovely pink drink, and was having a little bit of a hard time keeping up.

"Risa, you didn't ask for that to be virgin like I told you, did you?"

"I forgot."

Ben smiled even more broadly down at Risa, and started to take the seat next to her instead of Kristy, but was quickly foiled. Risa was relieved—Ben was supposed to be paying attention to Kristy, not her.

"Hey, sweet pea. I'm sorry I'm late."

They all looked up in surprise as Daniel appeared by the side of the table, leaning in to plant a kiss on Risa's cheek before sitting down. She was confused, but she enjoyed the feel of his lips again almost as much as the drink. When he moved away, though, she frowned.

"You aren't supposed to be here."

He smiled at Ben and Kristy in a knowing way, arching an eyebrow at the empty drink glasses. "I had some errands to run earlier but I thought you'd be home tonight."

"You did?" Risa knew something was off, but she was having a hard time thinking clearly.

"Uh-oh. Rum. You know it goes straight to your head."

"I do? It does?" she questioned, then reconsidered. "Yes, it does. It's very nice. I've never had anything go to my head before."

Daniel smiled and leaned in closer. "Except me, I hope."

His voice was low and suggestive, and Risa couldn't help smiling at him—somewhere in her head, a voice was telling her to stop smiling, but she couldn't seem to obey the internal command.

Ben, seeing that Risa was apparently spoken for, turned his attention to Kristy, and Daniel breathed a sigh of relief. He'd been watching from a dark alcove in the bar, and it was apparent Risa was heading for another troublesome situation. She didn't handle liquor well, or maybe she handled it a little too well—she was practically chugging her drink. He stalled her hand as she was reaching for the drink Kristy had left on the table now that Risa had drained her second one.

"I think you've had enough of those."

"Don't tell me what to do. You're not my boss. I don't have any bosses anymore. I can do what I want. I'm getting a life."

When she turned around on him, he drew back at the ferocity in her tone.

Daniel didn't argue, letting her sip the drink, her mutinous eyes meeting his over the top of the glass. He caught the waitress as she delivered the wings, and asked for some fries and two coffees to go with them— Risa needed food and caffeine.

"You do seem to just pop out of nowhere, Daniel," Kristy commented, obviously taking his measure.

"I thought I recognized your car in the parking lot, and took a chance."

He smiled at Kristy, but turned his gaze to Risa, who was too busy consuming wings to participate in the conversation. When Ben asked Kristy to dance, she appeared unsure if she should leave Daniel alone with Risa. Daniel began to reassure her, but was cut off by Risa herself.

"Go right ahead—you two have fun. Daniel and I are just going to catch up on the old days."

Daniel raised an eyebrow; she really was loose lipped with the effects of the alcohol, not to mention she was plowing through chicken wings like Henry the Eighth. Her eyes were a little glazed, and her cheeks flushed. She was even beautiful when she was three sheets to the wind.

Daniel shifted his attention lower to the smooth skin of her throat, and the pulse visible there. The plunging neckline of her dress issued invitations that she was very likely completely oblivious to. He wasn't, however. Neither was Ben, nor most other men in the bar. He'd arrived just in time. Averting his eyes to the food, he commented, "You and Kristy seem close. How long have you known her?"

"Since this morning."

"You've only known her a day?"

"Mmm-hmm. She got my groceries for me, but we never really talked." Daniel wasn't sure what that meant, and didn't have time to ask as Risa licked her fingers, crooning over the wings, "These things are great. How come we never got food like this on the job?"

Daniel just smiled; he was much more concerned with Kristy's sudden appearance and apparent influence over Risa. "Aren't you a little worried that Kristy has so quickly befriended you?"

Risa shook her head, and he liked the way the shiny cap of copper hair swept against her cheek when she did.

"No. She's good, trust me. She found my surveillance stuff, and completely was okay about it. I even told her a little bit about my work."

Every alarm in his head started clanging, and he took Risa by the shoulders. "Stop. Say that again. You *told* her?"

Risa pulled back. "Not everything, I mean, not that I was a—"

"Risa," he interrupted her sharply, "remember where you are. Anyone could hear you."

"Sorry. I didn't tell her the whole truth. Just what I needed to so I could smooth over the camera thing."

"What camera thing?"

Haltingly, Risa told him about being discovered by Kristy monitoring the apartment complex. Daniel closed his eyes and ran a hand over his face—this was exactly the kind of thing he feared. It did explain the purchases Jack had mentioned, however. But even if Risa hadn't turned, she was operating on borrowed time. Nasty people in the world would stop at nothing to know what she had in that pretty little head of hers, even if she didn't have her superhero powers any longer. It just made her all the more vulnerable. She needed to blend in, to keep a low profile, and instead she was getting into trouble every ten seconds.

Risa hadn't been trained as an agent, and apparently all it took to make her talk was a display of friendship and a few daiquiris. Jack White and his cronies had been completely irresponsible throwing her out into the world. She was defenseless, and possibly dangerous to every agent she'd every worked with. She didn't need to switch allegiances; just one innocent slip up could mean disaster. Hopefully, it hadn't already.

"You're sure she doesn't suspect the truth?"

She shook her head. The waitress delivered the rest of the food. Risa looked at the coffee questioningly.

"What's that?"

"Something to help sober you up."

She eyed the daiquiri glasses longingly, but picked up the coffee cup. "So, do you want to tell me what you're doing here?"

With Kristy out of earshot, Risa's request was matter-of-fact. She was openly suspicious as she crossed her arms over her chest and pinned him with that beautiful blue glare.

"I'm just here to see how you're doing."

"That's it? I thought…I was wondering if you'd…" She stopped herself, looking down.

"What did you think, Risa?"

"I thought you might be here to tell me they wanted me back."

He blinked, startled by the vulnerability and the raw appeal in her eyes. Had she always been this beautiful? How could he not have noticed? Of course, she had too much alcohol in her system, so she wasn't as in control of herself as she'd normally be.

She thought he was here to bring her back into service? Before he could think of a response, she spoke quickly, filling the silence,

"I'd asked Dr. Laslow about retraining me for field work, you know, as a regular agent. He wouldn't hear of it. He said I'd been through enough and should just go enjoy life, but what is there to enjoy? I don't know how to do any of it. You know, normal things."

"I'm sure that's not true." Daniel didn't know what he'd expected, but it wasn't this floodgate of emotion and questions. She'd wanted to stay with the agency and retrain? And Laslow had refused her? He supposed the doctor had his reasons, but if Risa had wanted to stay with the agency, wouldn't that have been a viable way of retaining her loyalty and avoiding the situation they were in now? He made a mental note to check out the reasons Risa's request was denied.

"I hate it. Shopping, making friends, the things that other people do every day and *we* don't."

We. She felt a connection with him, a link to the only world she'd known, one that had made sense to her. He could use that. She'd allowed him to see a weakness, an opening for him to get inside her life and find out what he needed to know.

"I'm not here to rehire you, Risa." He ignored how the stricken disappointment on her face plucked at him. "But Jack White asked me to see how you were adjusting. To do what I could to help while I'm here visiting my family."

"So, that woman, the pregnant woman, she really was—"

"My sister? Yes. The youngest of five of us."

She turned away, and Daniel waited for her to process what she'd been told.

"I don't know what to do. I'm making a mess of it. I don't belong anywhere."

The way she spoke the words, in a voice coarse with sadness, he had no choice but to think she was being sincere, maybe even more so with her inhibitions lowered. Either way, Jack was right; they had a problem. In this psychological condition, Risa would be ripe for the picking if someone came along and offered her something to hold on to. It might as well be him.

"Let me help, Risa. I know the area, I know people here. They were wrong—Laslow, the rest of them—to just throw you out into the world and expect you to adjust."

"I don't think I can. I feel cut off from everything, nothing is right." Tears spilled down her cheeks, and he suspected the Risa Remington he'd stood by out in the field would be completely mortified by that show of weakness if she were sober, but at the moment, she let them fall without even raising a hand. He reached over, rubbing one from her cheek with the pad of his thumb. Her skin was like satin, and he had a hard time pulling his hand away.

"Believe me, sweetheart, you're not as different as you think you are. We all screw it up. Every day."

He studied her face, was drawn by the seductive curiosity in her eyes.

"Is that what you did? Screwed up?"

"What do you mean?"

"When you kissed me today."

"Do you want an apology?"

She looked at him closely. "No. I want…"

He was almost afraid to ask. "What?"

Her eyelashes were impossibly thick, and seemed to brush the soft skin of her cheek when she looked down, then up again.

"I think I'd like you to do it again."

He took a deep breath, more affected than he wanted to be by her words.

"You're drunk."

"Less than I was an hour ago. I know what I'm saying. Don't treat me like a child."

She rose abruptly and walked toward the door, and he barely had time to throw some bills on the table and follow her before she was already in the parking lot.

"Risa, wait." He trailed her to the car he'd seen her drive away in with Kristy, and grabbed her wrist. "It's cold—don't you have a jacket?"

The icy glare she shot in his direction stopped him short. Maybe he did sound as if he were treating her like a child, though he hadn't meant to.

"Here, take mine." He slipped the leather jacket off and handed it to her. She took it and pulled it on—it dwarfed her, making her look smaller, more vulnerable. Good. Perhaps that's what he needed to keep temptation at bay. It would be so easy to take her up on her offer, but it would also be wrong. She was inebriated, and Daniel didn't take advantage of women in that state. Not sexually, anyway. However, if he could use this to get inside her apartment, that was a different matter.

"Let me take you back to your place."

With a flirty look, she stepped closer, running her hand lightly down the front of his chest.

"Don't you want to know why I want you to kiss me, Daniel? I haven't liked anyone touching me since the accident, but you're different."

In spite of his best efforts, she'd hooked him.

"Why?"

"When I touch people now, I feel nothing, see nothing. It's like everything around me is dead, and I feel disconnected from the world. Unsafe, alone." She stepped even closer. "Yet when you touched me, when you kissed me, I didn't feel that way. It was…different."

"Different how?" Did he really want to wander down this path of questions? Too late.

"Warm, safe. For the first time in months, I felt connected to someone. Like I could almost feel what was going on inside of you, too."

"Do you mean you could read me? Are your powers active?" His mind froze, and he grabbed her shoulders. But she shook her head.

"No, no. Not like that. It was just…there was *something*. I could feel things, through your kiss. Not literally, like before, but in a different way."

She reached up, feathering her fingers over his lips, and he tried to reason. She couldn't read him, he realized with no small bit of relief—if she could, there was no way she'd be getting this close to him right now. She was sexually inexperienced—kissing him was just another way for her to connect with her old life, who she was.

"It was my first one, you know."

"First what?" He'd lost track. He was an experienced CIA operative, he'd been in hundreds of life-and-death situations, taken on missions that made action movies look like comic books, and yet here he stood, completely undone by the touch of a woman's hand.

"First kiss. When you kissed me in the store, that was the first time anyone's kissed me since my parents were alive. It was the absolute first time a man has kissed me."

Her sad confession was also an invitation, and one he found hard to resist; he closed his hand around hers and pulled her closer.

"Dammit, Risa." He shook his head, knowing it was wrong, but knowing he had to do it anyway. "That wasn't nearly special enough to qualify as a first kiss."

"It wasn't?"

"No. It was just for show, to shut you up before you got yourself in more trouble. So let's try again."

He went in slow this time, taking in her features. The dim light from the bar's neon sign gave her an almost otherworldly glow. Her hair was like silk, and he closed his eyes for a second at the erotic softness of it as he pushed it back from her face, observing the gentle slope of her jaw as he traced his hand along its line. Her lips were parted and short, expectant breaths asked him to hurry, but he wasn't going to hurry. Not this time. This wasn't a put-on for whoever was watching, not a cover for his mission. It was just him, Daniel MacAlister, kissing a woman who had never been properly kissed before, and wanting to do it right.

When he finally took her mouth, she still tasted of

strawberries, and lime…and sheer, female lust. It was intoxicating, and she leaned into him again in that soft, pliable way that made him instantly hard. He couldn't remember ever having such a hair-trigger reaction to a woman. He reminded himself to take care, to go slow, but the delighted moan that she let go into his mouth made it difficult. Her kiss drove him to imagine what she'd be like naked, underneath him, and the desire was so sharp to find out that he groaned.

"Open more for me, Risa. Let me in," he whispered against her lips, and she did as he requested, her head falling recklessly back onto the arm he'd wrapped around her shoulders as he tasted the sweeter, darker secrets of her mouth.

She was a quick study, kissing him back with fervent desire, open need. It was his turn to groan again, the sound of desire pulled from the deepest parts of him, echoing between them as he lost himself in the kiss, barely noticing how tightly her hands gripped his waist.

He didn't care if he ever breathed again, and the realization of how lost he was, how deeply affected the kiss left him, made him pull back abruptly, breaking the contact with startling quickness. She stumbled, falling against him. He steadied her, trying to catch his breath, looking around, trying to excuse his less than suave behavior.

"I thought I heard someone come out."

She was at least as affected as he was, her face flushed. He couldn't stop himself from reaching forward one more time, cupping her cheek, trying to reassert his calm.

Risa was dangerous. Maybe not in the way the CIA feared, but she was like a drug. He licked his lips, watched hers and wanted nothing more than to taste her again.

"Hey, is everything okay? Risa?"

Kristy's voice broke the spell, and they stepped apart as she and Ben approached. It helped clear Daniel's mind, and he reminded himself to do much more thorough background checks on both of them. He also needed to check out the surveillance Risa had mentioned—what was she up to back in that apartment of hers? And how much did Kristy really know?

"I'm fine," he heard Risa reassure her friend, and was amazed that she'd recovered more quickly than he, sounding perfectly normal.

"Risa, I was kind of hoping, if you two are good, that maybe Daniel could give you a ride home? Ben's asked me to a party."

Before Risa could speak, Daniel reassured Kristy and Ben that was fine—he was happy to take Risa back to her place. To Kristy's credit, she waited until she had a solid okay from Risa, too.

Daniel's mind clicked back into work mode as they walked to his car. Taking Risa home would give him a chance to check out her apartment, at the very least— not to be seduced by Risa, but to find out if she posed a significant threat or not. After that, he had to stay away from her, because one thing was for sure: whether Risa was dangerous in her capacity as a former superhero and government agent or not, he knew that getting too close to Risa the woman posed a serious threat to him.

5

RISA GROANED as she rolled over, worried for a moment that she was heading into another one of her blackouts. But this time, the headache just seemed to be a garden-variety one, accompanied by a sick feeling in her stomach. Having never been ill, except for the collapses that followed some of her overloads, every brand-new sensation was burning itself into her brain with enthusiastic intensity. Her head spun when she lifted it. Was this how people felt when they had the flu? Could she have gotten a virus at the bar?

She sat up, slowly, swinging her legs over the side of the bed, noting that she still had her pretty dress on. It was wrinkled and misshapen after sleeping in it all night, but that was the least of her worries as her stomach turned once, violently, as soon as her feet hit the floor.

Balancing carefully as she stood, she was sure she'd never felt this weak in her life. Her bones were liquid, and her hand shook as she raised it to her face.

Suddenly she had the worst sensation; a sense of complete, impending doom overtook her as her skin became clammy and cold. She let out a small moan, bolting to the bathroom and heaving over the toilet. As her stomach rebelled, she sank to her knees, tears coming to her eyes. This was revolting! What was happening to her? She felt helpless, sick and disgusting.

Catching her breath, she stood again and stripped down, heading directly for the shower and bringing her toothbrush and paste with her. The heat of the shower, and getting this disgusting taste out of her mouth, was what she craved.

Risa didn't emerge for twenty minutes, brushing her teeth for at least ten of those. She still felt terrible, but the worst of the sickness appeared to be over. Her skin was pink from the hot water, the blotches on her cheeks accentuating her paleness when she looked in the mirror. However, she could stand without trembling now. Grabbing a terry cloth robe from the back of the door, she shrugged it on, letting it wick up the moisture she was too tired to dry away. This seemed to be her week of firsts. First friend, first bar, first illness, and first...

"Oh, no...what did I *do?*"

She wasn't pale anymore as the heat flamed in her cheeks and she raised her fingertips to her mouth.

The kiss.

She'd practically begged Daniel to kiss her. And he had—the sensations came flooding back, and she sank down onto the bench by the vanity. Daniel had kissed her—she remembered him saying the kiss at the store hadn't been a proper first kiss, so he'd corrected that. Dropping her head into her hands, she was mortified as every humiliating detail returned in excruciatingly clear color and sound.

The pink drinks.

The pink drinks were responsible for this. They'd tasted so good, appealing to her sweet tooth, but she'd had no idea they would affect her so dramatically. Realization sunk in—it was the pink drinks that were making her sick. They were harmless looking, delicious...and they were poison. She should have known, but she'd felt so out of her element, so awkward and desperate to leave—until that pink drink had saved her.

With a groan, she stood, attempting to convince herself to be glad that it wasn't more serious. The alcohol in the drinks had poisoned her system—and she was feeling the effects. It was to blame for everything...even the kiss.

She felt marginally better as she stood, and her stomach growled. She would see if she could take some toast. Or maybe a few spoonfuls of chocolate pudding.

As she opened the bathroom door, the sound filling the room confused her for a moment, until she realized what it was—her phone was ringing. Her phone never rang—who would call her?

She ignored her throbbing head as she searched for her bag, trying to follow the direction of the sound, missing the old days when she could have sensed the presence of the device and walked to it without doubt, and discovered who was seeking her with a touch. Finally, victoriously, her hands closed around the small, slim receiver.

"H-hello?"

"Hey, it's me. Kristy. I was about to come up there."

Risa blinked, unsure how to respond to the obvious

concern in Kristy's voice. "I couldn't find my phone. How did you get my number?"

"I programmed it into my cell last night—don't you remember? Before you left with Daniel, I made sure I got it. But I guess your memory might be a little fuzzy at the moment? Hmm?"

Kristy sounded bubbly and energetic as always, and Risa sank on the bed, wondering if the woman ever had a bad day. She didn't remember giving Kristy the phone number, but there were gaps, apparently; she wasn't exactly sure what she did or didn't remember.

Except for the kiss. That was firmly etched in her mind.

"Are you okay? Do you need me to come up? You sound a little froggy. Hungover, huh?"

Risa groaned. "Yes. Yes, that's it. Hungover. How long does this last?"

"The worst of it won't last too long—you didn't drink all that much."

"Oh, okay. I'm okay. No need to come over."

"Do you have company, by any chance?"

Risa frowned, walking to the fridge and pulling out a bottle of water. If she were hungover, then she was dehydrated. She took a drink before answering.

"No, why would I?"

"Well, you and Daniel seemed pretty hot for each other last night. I was a little worried about leaving you with him, but it sounds like you're fine."

"He was fine. I don't remember much."

"Well, you were slugging back those drinks like a champ."

"Apparently." Risa closed her eyes, trying to will away the pain.

"Take aspirin—it'll help. Then ask me."

"Ask you what?"

"About Ben!"

Risa sighed, getting to her feet and realizing she was probably going to have to eat something while on the phone. Kristy didn't appear to be winding down anytime soon.

"What about him?"

"Well, just as I suspected, he's sexy, classy and God, his kisses just set my toes on fire."

"That sounds uncomfortable."

Risa heard a snorting noise on the other side of the line. "Yeah, like you weren't sizzling from head to foot—and every inch in between, by the way—plastered up against Daniel last night."

Great. They'd been kissing in public; her humiliation was complete. "I was drunk. I didn't know what I was doing."

"Looked like fun, anyway. And it seems like you might have a potential solution for your little problem."

"What problem?" Risa grabbed two pudding cups and some canned whipped cream and sat down, wishing she could just eat some breakfast.

"Being a virgin, hon—Daniel looks like he could solve that problem very nicely indeed."

Risa almost dropped the pudding cup on the floor. "I don't think so."

"Why not? He'd be perfect. He has that look, you

know—experienced, the kind of guy who knows his way around a woman's body. Believe me, that's what you want the first time."

"I don't think I'll be seeing him again."

"Don't let that happen. You should call him."

Risa started to object, but thought about the kiss again. Contrary to what she told Kristy, she did remember most of what happened the previous evening. Daniel had been very nice to her—and the kiss had made an impression that branded itself on her mind permanently. His lips had fit hers perfectly, and she'd wanted nothing more than to experience that feeling—warm, complete, connected— for as long as possible. She couldn't deny that she wanted more. But to have sex with him? She didn't know if she wanted to have sex at all, ever.

"I don't think he wants that, either. He was just being nice."

"Oh, honey, men aren't that nice unless they have other things in mind. And he didn't take advantage of you when you got home. I would find him and jump him just for that. Imagine, he's a gentleman on top of everything else."

Risa blinked, moving into the front room after disposing of her empty pudding cups. Sitting down at her computer station, she frowned when she didn't see the hallway scan and started checking, furiously hitting buttons.

"It's all gone," she whispered, finding only ordinary software. Her surveillance system had been wiped. Daniel might not have taken her virginity, but he did take all of her surveillance equipment.

"He took everything."

Kristy gasped on the other side of the phone. "He *stole* from you? I take it back. He's a rat—what did he take? It's not like you had a lot there... What could he possibly have wanted?"

Temper renewing her sense of purpose, she spoke with grim determination. "I don't know—but I'm going to find out."

"I CAN'T SAY FOR SURE, Mom. I'll try to make it. Things have gotten...unexpectedly busy here. But I'll try, I really will."

Daniel drove into the parking lot of his motel, biting back a sigh as his mother exerted pressure akin to that he'd experienced two hundred feet below the ocean's surface. Daniel had spent the day at the local community college, using their public labs to filter through some of the recordings that Risa had stored on her system—the one he'd been up half the night disassembling—and he was beat. His resistance was low, and while the CIA had taught him various ways to handle interrogations and torture, they hadn't included Dorothy McAlister's methods in their repertoire.

He stepped out of the car and leaned against the side, conflicted. He enjoyed hearing his mother's voice—he thought of her every day—but fought the maelstrom of memories the contact was stirring up.

"Dad won't want me there, Mom. It's his birthday. He should have a good day. Not be reminded of all...that."

His mother's tone softened. She insisted his father

had missed him as much as she did, and that he was proud of him—Daniel found that hard to believe. To say they'd parted on bad terms was a grand understatement. He knew coming home would only upset his father. After all, Arthur MacAlister held Daniel responsible for his son's death. Daniel accepted that—in his heart, he held himself responsible for what had happed to Stewart, too.

"Okay, Mom. I'll think about it. I promise."

He clicked off the call, feeling hollowed out in a way he hadn't in many years. A part of him wanted what he'd given up, what he'd walked away from. But he didn't feel as if he "fit" anymore. He'd lived a life that was completely foreign to them. The CIA was his life, and he'd done things in the course of his work that his mother wouldn't like to think her boy was capable of. On the other hand, his father probably wouldn't be surprised at all to find out some of the lines Daniel had crossed over the years in order to protect his country.

Guilt, regret and too many other raw emotions that he'd left lying quietly for years had been stirred, and Daniel didn't like it. People depended on him to do what needed to be done. It wasn't always pretty. He couldn't afford guilt and regret; those things were an agent's worst enemy, stealing confidence and the ability to make hard decisions. Like the ones he had to make about Risa.

So far he'd found nothing to incriminate her, and he was glad for that—maybe more relieved than he should be. That was a problem, and he'd stayed away from her all day, trying to get his focus back. He'd almost accomplished that until he'd picked up the phone without thinking and discovered his mother on the other end—he'd been avoiding just this conversation.

Too many emotional triggers. Too many questions he didn't have answers for.

Shaking it all off, he inhaled the crisp, cleansing night air and popped up the steps to his room on the open second level of the inn. As he stepped inside, his instincts didn't kick in for a millisecond. It wasn't the first time he'd screwed up since returning to the Cape. It could have cost him his life under other circumstances.

What was going on with him? He should have noticed the light through the window before he'd even approached the door, should have remembered he didn't leave it on. Should have sensed her presence before he heard the sound of her moving in the corner.

As his hand reflexively slipped down to find the reassuring presence of his gun, he stilled when he saw her sitting under the dim light of the floor lamp that arched over the chair beside the bed, the files strewn at her feet, the questions raging in her eyes.

"Risa." The name whooshed out of him on the breath he'd been holding. She stood, her frame held taut. Angry. Frightened? The senses that alerted him to danger relaxed, just a bit.

"What are you doing here? How did you find me?"

"You aren't the only one who can spy on people, Daniel. I called your sister—they're in the phone book. They let me know where you are, your number. It was that easy." She gestured to the files on the floor. "The real question is, why do you have all this information on me? Where did you get it? Why are you really here?"

Her voice rose with the intensity of her questions, and he shut the door behind him, ensuring their privacy.

"Risa, calm down. Now."

She bent, picked up a handful of papers from the floor and crushed them in her small fist as she approached him.

"You lied. Why, Daniel? Why would they give you these files just to stop by and see if I was okay? You'll stop at nothing, even using your own family to get what you want."

The sarcastic sneer in her voice bit at him—she wasn't far off the truth, after all—but he remained cool. But part of him wanted to explain, wanted to make it right with her. "Risa—"

"What? What can you possibly say? You know more about me than I knew. What I can't figure out is why you have this information, why you're here. Though I have a few theories."

He took a step forward when she dropped the pages and raised a hand to her head, her pale brow creased as if she were in pain.

"Risa, are you all right?"

"Just a headache…just a stubborn hangover," she laughed, though it wasn't funny. "You sure managed to take advantage of last night, didn't you? When you got back to my apartment, was it even a choice whether to pursue what we'd started in the parking lot, or were you planning to search the place the entire time? I can't believe I was so stupid. It's all a sham, including the kissing."

He took a big breath and held his hand up. "Hold on. You passed out in my car, and I carried you up, put you to bed. Are you actually angry that I didn't take you to bed when you were falling-down drunk?"

"Oh, you took advantage, just not in that way."

That was true, he had to admit. There was no point in lying to her about it.

"Getting rid of that equipment was for your own good. The surveillance was a crutch. A way to avoid the world, not to mention invading the privacy of innocent people."

Her eyes widened, and her pupils looked dilated to him. He stepped in closer, concerned. Her hangover should have been long passed by now; could she have some adverse reaction to alcohol that he didn't know about? Did her different physiology respond to its influences more strongly? He couldn't remember reading anything like that in the files. He moved forward, she moved back.

"You stay there," she warned, though he knew there wasn't much she could do if he refused.

"Risa, you don't look well."

"Yeah, and you're really concerned about my welfare, aren't you? Why are you after me, Daniel? Did they send you because they regret saving me, letting me go? I know it has to be important if they would send *you* to handle it."

"Risa, you're getting hysterical, just calm down and we can talk…they sent me because I know you. We worked together. They thought familiarity would help."

"Help with what, exactly? What do you need to get so close for, Daniel?" She paused, and he could see her mind ticking through the possibilities. "They sent you to see if I was still playing on the right side. To—"

"Just stop, will you?" He raised his own voice now and it thundered in the small room, drowning out hers. He struggled to maintain control, taking a deep breath. She was unpredictable, and he had to calm her down.

"Risa, I told you the truth. I grew up here on the Cape, and Jack White sent me to check up on you. My family really does live here, that really was my sister. Jack gave me those files so I could appreciate the changes you were dealing with, and so that I could make sure you were…not compromised in any way. And he did advise me to help you adjust, if you were having trouble. I was supposed to destroy the files—I guess I should have. I'm sorry you had to see them."

She was silent for a beat, and blinked her eyes, her jaw dropping for a moment, then closing again. "You think I'd turn? After all I've done, after all that my family has done, they think I would do that? And if they sent you, then—"

"They didn't know what you would do, Risa—no one has faced this situation before. I think Jack called it right—you are in trouble, whether you admit it or not. First you were almost arrested, then you left yourself wide open last night. You've already told at least one person you only knew for a few hours some of your secrets, and you've been watching and manipulating your neighbors instead of trying to live even a semblance of normal life. What were we supposed to think?"

Her stunned silence filled the room, and he shook his head, looking at the ceiling, wanting to make her understand.

"Listen, I understand why you felt you needed to do what you did, but it has to stop. Your actions could draw attention to you. What would happen if there was a fire in your complex and law enforcement found all that surveillance equipment? Or what if you'd been arrested at the store, or too loose lipped with the wrong person at the bar? You've done some stupid things, Risa, but that's why I'm here. To keep you from doing something really stupid."

He wouldn't admit to her what she probably already suspected—Jack's orders to "remove the problem" if there was one. That possibility had dimmed almost from the start. His objective now was saving her, helping her. And he'd make her believe it.

She nodded blankly, but didn't say a word. He took a step closer, taking this moment to drive his point home, that he was here to help. He stopped short, noticing that her breath was shallow, her hands were shaking. She only had time to say one thing to him before crumpling.

"Daniel, I…"

THE ROOM WAS COLD and dark, and Risa's back stiffened at the tone of Dr. Laslow's voice—she *hated* being told what to do.

"Don't be belligerent, Risa. This is your duty."

She dug in, crossing her arms over her stomach, tired of always going along, of being good and doing what she was told. "I don't want to do any more! I don't like it. I don't like what I see. *Please* don't make me do it."

Dr. Laslow looked at her from over the top of his ever-present clipboard, seemingly oblivious to the tears that stung her eyes. Her heart held some hope as he turned away from the illuminated center of the dark cell, moving outside the thick door and away from the man she was supposed to be scanning. Was he actually going to listen to her this time? When they stepped into the hallway, her hopes sank. He'd just taken her out here to lecture her. Again.

"Risa, you have a duty to your country and it's very important that you be brave. That man in there—" Dr. Laslow pointed back at the door "—intends to kill many innocent people. People like him are the ones who killed your parents. So if you can't do this for me, Risa, or for your country, then you should do this to honor your parents. They never said no to a mission. They wouldn't want you to, either."

The tears threatened harder, but she somehow kept them in. She knew what would happen if she cried. Dr. Laslow would just tell her that twelve years old was too old for that kind of behavior.

"Risa, this is who you are. It's your destiny."

She nodded glumly as he stepped back and let her pass. She didn't want her mom and dad to be ashamed of her, to think she was a coward, just in case they could know, somehow. She remembered all the stories her mom had told her about Grandpa, who'd been the first to work for his country. He'd been brave, helping end the war with his volunteering—meaning he did it because he wanted to, not because he was forced to. *People with our abilities need to use them for the good of everyone,* her mom used to say.

She wished she could at least have some cool superhero name, and maybe an outfit, like they did on TV, but it didn't work that way in real life. Boring clothes, boring name. It sucked having a destiny. How she wished she could just be like everybody else!

She set her thoughts aside as she approached the scary-looking man strapped to the table. *He can't hurt me, he can't hurt me. He's all tied up,* she repeated to herself as she looked into dark eyes that watched her warily.

Tentatively, she put one hand up on his forehead, getting closer as he tried to turn away. "Don't be afraid. It doesn't hurt," she reassured him in her childish voice, using his language. She'd read so many thoughts, the languages were imprinted on her mind and she could speak them as if they were her own. The second she made contact with his skin, the images and sounds raced before her, much like watching a videotape of someone else's life and thoughts, but through their own eyes.

She saw a small house, two women wrapped in robes and scarves, several happy children running about. She smiled, watching them play for a moment. The men held themselves off, separate, glancing around furtively now and then, as if to see if anyone was listening. She noticed they sat in front of a door. There was some kind of chanting in the background, but she dismissed it; it wasn't important.

Scanning someone's thoughts was sometimes like walking into their dreams, her mother had taught her—images and events you saw were sometimes real, and sometimes they were symbols that only seemed real. You could tell a lot about a person by the state of their thoughts, sort of like how clean their house was.

There was chaos sometimes, too much noise, too many things happening at once, but this man's mind was very clear and straightforward. It made it easier for her as she walked toward the door he stood in front of. Instinct told her it was important. When people were keeping secrets, they often hid them well, even in their minds.

"That's where the secrets are hidden," she whispered to herself.

She stepped past the man and his hand reached out to grab her—she felt his alarm, but he couldn't stop her. She could go anywhere she wanted. Stepping through the door, she found herself in a cavelike place, but there were lights, tables and men gathered in small groups. She walked to the table, and through his eyes she looked down at papers with plans, scribbled writing and pictures.

She started reading out loud, knowing someone in the regular world would be recording her, gathering the information. His thoughts flowed from her lips like a stream of data, until she had read all of the visible papers.

Someone somewhere asked a question—someone in the room with her, and she waited. They were trying to find out more.

Suddenly, she found herself in a new setting, sitting in the backseat of a van, seeing everything again through the eyes of the man she was reading. Two other men sat, their coats bulky, their faces resolute. They talked of bombs, celebrations and their happiness at helping with their cause.

A few moments later the van stopped, the men stepped out and walked toward a crowded mall. They were going to kill all those people, she realized. Blow them up. It hadn't happened yet. He hadn't seen it, he was just imagining how it would be—there was still time. She searched the scene frantically for a date, a time. A clock tower said six o'clock…but what day? Children ran past her, playing. Adults sat talking, not knowing what was coming. Risa felt her mind merging with the man's, felt his hatred, his sense of purpose, his dark determination, and plunged even deeper, looking for when…

Finally, she saw a newspaper in someone's hand, but no matter how close she came, she couldn't find a date. She started asking everyone around her—when? *When?* The information had to be here somewhere. How had he hidden it? We have to stop them…

But there was no answer. Just images in his brain, memories, thoughts, wishes. Hateful, awful wishes. She heard the blast, saw the carnage and kept searching anyway. He was just imagining it, wishing for it…it wasn't real. Yet.

She felt someone pull her away but she wasn't going to let go…she had to find out when. They had to know when, or there was no way to save those people. Her mom had told her she had to help people.

"Get her off of him, *now!*" A voice from somewhere

else invaded. She felt a sharp sting in her arm, as her body jolted and she started to lose her grip on his thoughts, but she fought and fought, unwilling to let go until she could find the date…save the people.

When she was pulled free of the man, the connection broken, she thrashed out like a wild animal, furious they would stop her from finding out, and she struggled against the hands that held her down, several of them needed to restrain her even though the Taser shock had turned her muscles to jelly, while Dr. Laslow prepared a hypodermic.

"No! No! Stop! I have to find out *when!*" she wailed into the room, but the voice that answered her wasn't Dr. Laslow's. The hands that held her didn't feel like the hard, viselike grips of his assistants….

"Risa, it's me, it's Daniel. You're okay, you're okay. Settle down, you're safe."

6

"BUT I DIDN'T find out when…"

"When what?"

"When they planned the attack. When they would kill all the people."

Her voice still sounded like a child's, and for several minutes Daniel held her and rocked her like one, wondering what the hell had happened. She'd passed out, but shortly after she'd started thrashing and babbling in different languages, caught in a memory of the past. He'd realized he was witnessing firsthand the blackouts mentioned in the files. She'd fought him tooth and nail while he'd tried to restrain her, to keep her from hurting herself, if not him. If she'd still had her superpowers, he would have been in serious trouble.

As she quieted, he could feel her come back to herself, to the moment, and it was then that she disengaged herself, pulling away. He was reluctant to let go.

"What happened, Risa? Can you tell me?"

She wrapped her arms around her waist, going over to the window.

"It's been happening a lot since the accident. I get horrible headaches, blackout, and it's like I'm reliving things from my life. Nothing recent—sometimes they're okay, pleasant even, and other times, like this time…"

He nodded to show he was listening. "You said you couldn't find out when an attack was happening?"

She looked away from him. "A terrorist they'd captured—there was going to be a suicide bombing on a busy street, lots of cafés and stores, people everywhere. I could see it as he pictured it happening—as he'd hoped it would happen—but I couldn't find the date." She sighed, running her hands over her face, seeming to gather herself before continuing.

"I didn't know until later that information like that wasn't often known until the last minute. He knew it was going to happen, but he didn't know when. If *he* didn't know, there was no way for *me* to know. I could only see what was in his thoughts. His brother was one of the bombers and they were so happy about it, thrilled. But I couldn't save those people, because I couldn't find out when."

Daniel tried to calm the thudding of his own heart as he listened, trying to imagine what she'd been through, but knowing he couldn't even come close, for all of his own experience. "It wasn't your fault, Risa. None of it. How old were you?"

"Twelve."

He paused for a moment, absorbing that, keeping his voice steady. "When you were coming awake, you were fighting me—why? What was happening in your memory? Were you attacked?"

She curled into herself, like a wounded animal; it

made Daniel want to hold her again, but he knew he had to let her have her own space. If she were reliving an attack, she wouldn't need him closing in on her as she remembered.

"No, I wasn't attacked—just the opposite. I guess I flipped out when I couldn't find the date, and lost control. I started choking him, touching him harder, trying to find a way in, a deeper connection, I guess, and I almost killed him. I didn't mean to, but I got lost in his head, and my body just took over. They had to pull me off. Dr. Laslow had to sedate me. I was fighting against his assistants as they tried to hold me, so I guess that must have transferred to fighting you, if you were trying to do it, too. I hope I didn't hurt you."

Stunned by her explanation, Daniel ignored her concern about him. "They *drugged* you?"

Daniel stood—outraged, helpless, sick in his soul about what she'd been through—and there was nothing he could do. The files hadn't made any note of sedation or restraint, hadn't mentioned her being out of control. Laslow must have omitted certain items to protect his own hide. Questions would have been raised, for sure, had he included those details.

But Risa shrugged it off, to his astonishment. She didn't seem to think there was anything wrong with what had happened—had they so completely brainwashed her into thinking she was at fault? That she was responsible for a normal reaction, given the extraordinary circumstances?

"With my increased strength, they had no choice. I

was too strong, and I could have easily killed or hurt someone, even at that age. It didn't happen often. I learned more self-control over the years, how to reign in anger or frustration when I was scanning. But there were just some moments when it would get the best of me."

Her arms wrapped around her small frame even more tightly, and Daniel couldn't hold himself back anymore. He crossed the space between them, taking her deep inside his arms, wanting to cover her and protect her from those memories, useless as that was. She leaned in, seeming small, and he wished he could do more. How had Laslow allowed this to happen, or Jack? She'd been a child, and no one had protected *her.* He hadn't realized he'd spoken his thoughts aloud, and she pulled back, looked up at him sadly.

"It was *my* job to protect. Not theirs."

His hands closed over her shoulders, and he held her gaze.

"It was theirs, too. You were a child. You were parentless. You were never given the choices you should have been given. You're a human being, and an American citizen. Your rights were horribly violated."

"My family…"

"They were all consenting adults, and they had each other to rely on. Your grandfather probably helped protect your mother, but you were left alone, at Laslow's mercy. If I ever see that bastard again, I might just see how he enjoys being held down and—"

He stopped when he saw her eyes had gone wide, and she was staring at him like she'd never seen him before.

"He did what he had to do—he knew what was best."

Daniel slipped his palms from her shoulders to her soft, tear-stained cheeks and smoothed his thumb over the skin there. "No, he didn't. He did what was best for the agency, best for himself and his research but not best for a young girl who had no one else to depend on."

Her brow creased, as if she didn't understand how to deal with someone who was willing to protect *her*. Daniel didn't completely understand it himself. *Duty, mission, loyalty, focus*—those had always been his keywords. Mission above all else. It was how he lived his life. But at the moment, his focus on the mission was all but absent as the overwhelming impulse to protect Risa—to care for her, to keep her safe—took over.

He couldn't deny the desire to connect on every level, to get close and not let go. To make up for everything she'd suffered. A brief flash of guilt, of insight, regarding his brother Stewart rose in his mind, but he squashed it. He could never make things right for his brother, but he could for Risa.

"Risa, I want to help. You need to let me know how to do that."

She looked down, and the motion brought his hand into excruciating contact with the edge of her mouth. The contact zinged throughout his body like an electric shock. Amazingly, she did something he never would have expected in a thousand years.

She smiled.

"This helps. Being close to you helps. I'd like to be as close to you as possible, Daniel."

She stretched up as he bent down, and she whispered something in his ear. His heart nearly hit the floor at the quietly whispered request, and for the first time in many years, Daniel McAlister was faced with a situation he wasn't quite sure how to handle.

"Uh, hell, Risa." Daniel ran his hand through his hair, turning away, unsure about this unexpected complication. It would be far too easy to give in, to grant her wish and lose himself in the sweetness of her body, but he'd sworn he wouldn't cross that line. Of course, he hadn't expected her to issue any invitations, either.

When she circled around him, her hands sliding around his midsection from behind, splaying over his chest, the push of her breasts against the middle of his back had him instantly erect. The one million reasons he shouldn't do this were fading. What was it about her that completely destroyed his self-control, obliterating all of the carefully built discipline and skills that had always seen him through?

He swallowed hard when she kissed his shoulder blade, the sensation warm and sweet, even through his shirt. He was hard, he was ready, but it wasn't right— was it? He turned to face her, trying to put at least an arm's length of distance between them.

"Risa, I don't know why you think this is how I can help you, but you're playing with fire."

"I know what I want, Daniel. I know what's happening between us, even if I've never experienced it. I've read books, watched movies."

"That's hardly the same. This is a big deal, Risa. Your first time should be with someone special."

"Why?"

He blinked, surprised into silence, and maybe even a little insulted that she didn't respond that he *was* special. That he cared what she thought caught him doubly unaware. Some untapped pool of emotions, of thoughts and feelings, had been opened, and he found himself helpless to turn them off around her. His reply sounded lame to his own ears, even as he spoke it. "Well, just because it should. It's an important moment."

She looked at him curiously. "I like how you make me feel. You're the only person I can stand to touch. What if I can never touch anyone else? What if you're the only one I can feel comfortable with?"

The implications of her innocent statements should have had him escorting her to the door. But another thought played alongside his objections—what if she was right?

How could she ever expect to develop normal relationships if she never experienced it? He breathed in, considering his course of action. It was within mission parameters—Jack had made that clear. Yet, Daniel was conflicted because getting involved was completely different when you felt something. Usually work-related trysts were not about emotion—but he couldn't deny he felt things around Risa. Things he shouldn't be feeling. Still…

He didn't have to take it all the way, but maybe he could spend some time with her, show her how to relax, to enjoy a man's company. And if he were completely honest, he found the idea of her sharing herself with another man extremely…irritating. What if the guy was a jerk? What if he didn't make it good for Risa? She'd had enough bastards in her life.

Not that Daniel felt he could exactly exempt himself from that status, but he knew, deep down, that if she was going to be with anyone, he wanted it to be him. The idea of another man's hands on her wasn't something he cared to think about.

As he rationalized, he rubbed his thumb against the silky ridge of her collarbone, staring at her the entire time, though not seeing. When he refocused, he saw she was no longer pale; the flush in her cheeks was high, her blue eyes dark with expectation. As long as the ground rules were clear, maybe he could provide her with some pleasure, replace some of the painful memories of her past with hope for the future. He took a deep breath, committing to the moment before he could talk himself out of it again.

"I don't want to hurt you, and I don't mean only physically, though if there's anything you don't like, you should tell me…but you know I won't be here for good. You know I have to go back. You'll never see me again."

Risa felt her heart pound harder, the stress of the moment replaced with expectation as she nodded—she wasn't a child, she knew what she was asking. Though Kristy probably had been joking, she'd also had a point—Daniel *was* perfect. And Risa wasn't stupid. She knew there were hidden agendas at play, reasons Daniel was here that he wasn't telling her.

But at the moment, his thumb was sliding along her neckline in a very wonderful way. She wanted to forget all of the strategizing, forget the pain and the distrust. What she wanted more than anything was to just soak in this moment. She wanted him; she'd always wanted him.

"I know Daniel. That's okay… I'm a virgin, not an idiot."

He smiled at that, and she smiled back, catching her breath slightly when his hand drifted lower, just grazing her nipple before settling on her waist. It all felt so good, and impatience overcame her. She wished he would hurry, move faster, do more. She wanted to feel everything. *Now.* Before he changed his mind.

Then again, slow was good, too, she thought as he lowered his head, taking her bottom lip between his teeth and sucking lightly as his fingers teasingly caressed the underside of her breast. Though she tried to maneuver herself into his palm, he stayed in torturous control.

"You don't have to go so slowly, I know what is supposed to happen, I want it—"

"Stop being so bossy. I want to enjoy this, too… You're delicious, do you know that? I could lick you from head to toe. Slowly. In fact…"

He chuckled against her mouth as he spoke, and she shivered at the husky playfulness in his voice. Somehow she'd thought he'd be more task oriented, like he was on the job. But Daniel was revealing more to her than he probably knew. She stiffened for a moment, the thought chilling her—what was it exactly that she was feeling? Why did she feel so much around him? Was he revealing things or was she sensing them?

And if so, how?

He pulled back, and she blinked, feeling the panic subside—normal people could pick up on each other's moods, right? Just because she could sense something about Daniel didn't mean her powers were coming back. She tried to calm her thoughts.

"Are you okay? Do you want me to stop?"

She'd never heard him sound so sexy before, so intimate, and she liked it. A lot. She shook her head, embarrassed about her lapse—stopping was the last thing she wanted him to do. Doubts were erased with that realization. She caught her breath as he dipped down and lifted her shirt in one swift move, moving his tongue over the skin of her stomach in a wet swipe. Her knees wobbled. She'd never been touched like this, never knew it could be so powerful. The melting sensation took over as her insides seemed to go liquid.

She buried her hands in his hair more for balance than to direct him, but he growled his approval at her touch as he ripped her bra aside for better access. He closed his lips over the tip of one breast and she pressed him closer. He rubbed his tongue against her raised flesh and sucked until she keened with pleasure, arching into the sensation.

"You like that?" he murmured roughly, his breath feathering over her skin.

Like? she thought. Such a weak word for how she felt about his mouth on her.

"I want more. Don't stop."

"Furthest thing from my mind…"

Risa soon forgot everything but the increasing sense of urgency, as thousands of new sensations assaulted her body as he kissed her everywhere. She tried to experience them each separately, but it was impossible as they all swirled together into one blur of pleasure.

His hand trailed along the inside of her thigh, and she caught him, clenching tightly, the urges he triggered overwhelming. Her jeans were only unbuttoned at the top where he'd dipped his tongue into her belly button, his wet kisses sending every nerve ending into a frenzy.

When he pressed his hand against her crotch, rubbing the seam of the thick denim against her center, she moved against him shamelessly, following his lead.

"Good?" he asked, the other hand planted firmly on her backside, keeping her still while his mouth went to her other breast.

"Mmm-hmm…I want my jeans off…they're in the way."

"This is fine for now."

"But…"

"You'll see…stop talking," he commanded softly, his breath dancing over the skin of her belly. She never would have thought such a light sensation could be so intense.

She gazed down at Daniel—a man she knew was powerful and feared—kneeling by her feet, caressing her with his hands and his lips. He stood and pulled her over the bed by her hand, and she followed willingly, wondering what was next. He leaned back, looking at her for long, hot moments, and the dreaded heat crept back into her face.

"Stop looking at me like that." She turned her head away, but he gripped her chin and made her face him.

"I enjoy looking at you—you're beautiful, especially like this."

"Can't you just keep touching me?"

As he stretched out beside her in a smooth move, he slipped his arm beneath her neck for support, kissing her again with wide open, consuming kisses that drugged her. Led by curiosity and desire, she reached down and found him, testing the hardness of him through his pants. His body wrenched, and he moaned at the unexpected touch. She drew her hand away quickly. He replaced it.

"Sorry, you just took me by surprise. You can touch me anywhere you want...especially there."

She reached down again, relieved he liked it, measuring him in her hand, amazed at the full, rock-hard length of him. She became bolder, and slipped her hand inside his jeans, hoping she wouldn't make him jump again. She found the silky hardness of his cock even nicer to touch without barriers.

"You feel so good, so much better than I ever imagined. I love touching you."

He groaned at her confession, rocking into her hand, "I want to touch you the same way, Risa...."

He burrowed his hand down inside of her jeans, and she cried out when the touch of his skin met hers in a place she'd only imagined being touched. His long fingers stroked and explored between her thighs as he continued to kiss her with increasing demand. Words and talking were left behind in a haze of moans and sighs. She strained against his fingers as they pressed and rubbed and kissed until her body arched of its own volition, her lips ripping away from his with a soundless scream as the pleasure ripped through her, stealing her breath.

Not wanting it to stop, she chased every last vestige of the elusive pleasure, moving against him even more eagerly. He groaned against her breasts, his hot breaths deepening as he pushed rhythmically into her grip, showing her what he wanted her to do. His hand left its intimate nest inside her jeans as his arms banded around her and he buried his face in her neck, growling as he came, hot and slick in her palm. She kept massaging him, not wanting it to end. As the moment passed, they disengaged and both lay back, letting their labored breathing settle.

Risa watched him quietly until his eyes also shifted to meet hers. She felt as if she should say something, but she wasn't exactly sure what. The obvious popped out of her mouth first,

"Thank you, Daniel."

"My pleasure, Risa."

There was a new lightness in his voice when he responded, and she couldn't help but smile.

"I always wondered what it felt like, to have an orgasm. It's amazing—you made it amazing."

He propped up on one elbow, looking down at her,

and traced her lips with his forefinger, on which she could still detect the muskiness of her own scent. The warm feeling that had preceded her first orgasm started curling in her midsection again. Without thought, she moved her mouth, grasping his finger between her lips, sucking the salty tip, enjoying his grunt of approval as her gaze glued on to his. Daniel seemed to enjoy her touch as much as she enjoyed his, she marveled.

"It'll get even better, believe me." His voice was unsteady when he responded. Was he feeling the same things she was?

"I believe you," Risa whispered.

"You've never had an orgasm before? Even self-initiated?"

Shrugging, she drew her finger back. "I tried it a few times, but I must have been doing something wrong, because nothing happened. It just felt weird. I thought my body just wasn't built for it."

He laughed, standing and offering a hand to help her up. "Believe me, your body is definitely built for it."

His praise, the things he said, and the way he looked at her made her want to stay naked in front of him for as long as possible. Though she'd felt exposed and unsure when he'd looked at her so intently just moments ago, now she liked the way his eyes moved from her eyes to her mouth to her chest—and how his lips parted as if he wanted to taste her again.

She felt powerful, and…attractive. Her mind drifted back to remember some of the underwear that Kristy had tossed in her shopping bag. Until now, she hadn't seen the point of it, but she wondered what Daniel would think if she wore some of the silky scraps.

"You keep looking at me like that, Risa, and we may never make it out of here." He picked up her shirt just as the phone rang, startling them both. Daniel made no effort to answer it, and in seconds, his sister's voice filled the room.

"Daniel? Are you there? Daniel? Okay…well then, whether you are there or not, Mom said she invited you to the party tomorrow night, and I wanted to add my voice to hers. You should come—Dad will want you there. I know it's difficult with Stewart, but you two need to mend fences. Mom agreed you should bring Risa, too. I already invited her earlier when she called looking for you, but maybe coming together might make it more fun. Tomorrow night, seven sharp, brother. Be there."

And with that, the machine clicked off, and a tense silence took over the room. Risa pulled her shirt slowly over her shoulders as Daniel raised himself from the floor and walked away from her without a word.

"Who's Stewart?"

Her question rang sharply in the room. He didn't answer. His back was turned toward her as he looked out through the small gap in the curtains to the dark parking lot below. She stood up, too, unsure what to say or do next, and tried to reassure him in the only way she knew, trying to close the gap between them.

"I didn't plan on going, of course. You don't have to worry about that," she said.

Still, no answer. She set her lips together, hating how

well and truly he'd shut her out after they'd been so close. Why did the stupid phone have to ring? If his stupid sister hadn't called, they'd be touching each other again instead of standing on opposite sides of the room. Risa went to the door, but when her hand turned the doorknob, she found his quickly covering it, stopping her.

"Where are you going?"

She looked back over her shoulder, and he was there, standing so close that, if she just leaned in a little, she could kiss him again. The temptation was strong.

"You want to be alone. I'll go back to my place."

His hand stayed on hers, the warmth of it softening the frustration she'd felt a moment ago.

"You shouldn't walk back by yourself. It's starting to rain."

"I'll be okay."

He paused for a moment, and then finally removed his hand, stepping back just slightly.

"Risa, I don't want you to go…."

Her breath caught a little when she noticed he hadn't buttoned his jeans back up.

"Well, I don't want to go—I mean, you want to be alone now. There'll be more time for…that." She eyed him speculatively. "Won't there?"

"Don't you want answers to your questions?"

"If you wanted to answer them, you would have."

He stepped a little closer, running a hand over his face, and she could see him smiling. "You're an unusual woman, Risa, former superhero status aside. But you don't have to go. We should get some food. We'll get something, and I can at least give you a ride back so you don't get soaked to the bone."

She fought the disappointment that he wasn't interested in having more sex. There was a dull thud of pain in her chest; she'd never felt it before. It hurt that he didn't want to be with her, but she wasn't going to let him know that. Even if they were just eating, spending time with Daniel was far more appealing than going back to her lonely apartment—and it hit her she'd never thought of her sanctuary that way before. It had been safe, not lonely, until recently.

"Okay."

He nodded and moved back toward the small bathroom. Her eyes fell on the papers she'd left scattered on the floor—suddenly it all seemed meaningless. It was her past—but none of it felt as real as Daniel's hands on her skin. That was all she could think about at the moment.

He left the door open, clicking on the light. She watched with her heart in her throat as he threw his pants outside the door, and she heard sounds of a suitcase opening and closing. He was naked, just yards away from her, all she had to do was close the distance…. Within moments, he stepped back out, wearing only close-fitting black briefs that didn't leave much to the imagination. She couldn't quite take her eyes away, and she wanted badly to touch him, but she was rooted to the spot, staring.

He stopped, searching through a drawer for another pair of pants, and turned his head to look at her.

"Does this bother you?"

"No." Her voice was husky, her breathing feeling short again, the warmth of his gaze invading her. "I just...I want..."

He slipped the pants on, zipping them quickly, walked over and took her into his arms. She could feel him against her stomach, hard again, and she shuddered, burying her face in his chest, inhaling his scent.

"Make no mistake, Risa. I want you, too. But not right now. Let's take it slowly, we have some time." He drew back, looking more serious. "Anna was right. It would be good for you to come to the party."

"How so?"

"You could meet people, enjoy yourself. My family, regardless of my issues with them, are nice people. You'd like them. They'd like you."

"I don't know, Daniel, what if they think—"

"That you and I are a couple? We are, now, aren't we? At least for a while?" He ran his hand down the length of her arm. "It would give us some time together, as well."

She shivered at the touch, feeling confused, seduced, happy, but cautious. She wanted Daniel, but she hadn't counted on getting involved, on meeting his family— didn't that mean something important? Getting to know someone's family?

"Listen, no pressure, but I think you'd have a good time. It'll be good for you to know people here. They can help you out after I go, if you need anything."

"Sure," she answered automatically, not really sure at all, but for some reason, she couldn't say no. She decided to push back a little bit, after all. "But if I'm going, and if we're a couple, they'll assume you've talked about them to me—can you tell me who's who? Like Stewart? Is he someone you don't get along with?"

He pulled away and she felt the chill between them again, but as he reached for a jacket on the chair, he sighed.

"There's not much to it, really. Stewart was my twin, and he died ten years ago. My father blames me. We argued—I left and didn't go back. It was the best thing for all of us. End of story, really."

Risa wasn't sure how to respond to the tightly controlled declaration, and his tone made it clear the topic wasn't open for general discussion, so she let it drop, stepping through the door when he opened it for her. As she fell into step beside Daniel on their way to the car, it was comforting to know that she wasn't the only one with demons in her past.

7

FRUSTRATED, Risa exited from yet another charming store filled to the ceiling with trinkets, local art and nautical items. Though she'd been looking all morning, she had absolutely no idea what to buy Arthur MacAlister for his birthday. Daniel said she didn't have to bring anything, but it seemed like the right thing to do when you were invited to someone's home. She wasn't entirely clueless, after all. She knew how to be polite.

No sooner had her foot hit the sidewalk than she was plowed into from the left side, setting her off balance and almost into the cast-iron rail running along the front of the shop, but for a pair of strong arms that reached out and broke her fall.

Regaining her balance, she looked up into Ben Richter's blue eyes. Beach-boy blond hair fell over his wide forehead, and a spark of recognition fired in his expression as he smiled. The guy was built like a line-backer, all muscle. If he hadn't grabbed her, she would have been badly hurt.

"Risa! I'm so sorry—I should have been looking where I was going. I was lost in thought. Are you okay?"

His voice was deep, and in spite of his accent, his

English was clear and flawless. Risa nodded, remembering the last time she'd seen him—when she'd been drunk at the bar. She extricated herself from his grasp.

"Hello, Ben. I'm okay. I was just shopping."

She nearly groaned at how stilted and lame her response was—of course she was shopping! Why else would she be stepping out of the boutique? But Ben, who towered over her, taller even than Daniel was, just smiled.

"Apparently you're not finding what you're searching for?"

"Hmm?" Risa realized a moment later that, for all of her efforts, she held no shopping bags, and that Ben had noticed. "Oh. No. I need a birthday present, for Daniel's father, but I've never met him, and I have no idea what to buy. I've never met any of his family, or even been to a big birthday party before, so I just have…no…idea." She wound down, unsure why she was babbling. But Ben chuckled, and didn't drop eye contact.

"Maybe I could help—give you a male perspective, at least."

"Don't you have to work?"

"Several members of my team are out of town to a conference in Boston today, so I was just taking a walk, enjoying the day. I have nothing planned, if you don't mind the company, of course."

Risa saw no reason to disagree, though as he fell in step with her on their way to the next shop, she felt strange. Her life was suddenly filled with people: first Kristy, then Daniel and his family, now Ben.

She watched him walk, weaving along the sidewalk

effortlessly, and remembered how gracefully he'd moved while practicing his martial arts—of course, she couldn't say she knew about that.

He kept smiling over at her. Was it normal for a man you barely knew to offer to help you shop? Was she being too friendly? Was he? What would Daniel think if he saw them out together? Would Kristy be upset, or get the wrong idea? Risa had no idea how these things worked.

She applied logic, the only reliable alternative to confusion. It wasn't as if Daniel had made any commitment beyond sleeping with her—and they hadn't even done that, not really. He wouldn't care, and even if he did, it was none of his business whom she spent her time with. But Kristy was a different matter—she was a friend. Risa didn't know all the rules, but she knew friends didn't go out with each other's boyfriends.

She looked up at Ben again, inquiring, "Why aren't you spending the day with Kristy?"

Something in his face changed. But his voice was warm when he spoke—Risa could see he liked her friend, but he didn't appear entirely comfortable with that fact.

"I would love to spend more time with her. Unfortunately, she did have to work today, though I may seek her out tonight for dinner."

She slowed her step, curious about what Ben would have to say about Kristy. Risa was discovering that she was an inquisitive person, more than she would have thought. Asking people questions served a practical purpose—if they were talking about themselves, they couldn't pry into her life.

"You two hit it off, then?"

Ben nodded slowly. "You could say that. She's very different from the women I usually date, but I like her very much."

"Different how?"

"Younger. Less…sophisticated, I suppose. The women I know in Germany are more serious, older. But Kristy is refreshing. And she's very attractive, of course. Very…American."

Risa smiled. "I happen to know she likes you, too. Very much."

Ben sighed heavily, holding the door for her as they walked into a small gallery together. "I don't want to give the wrong idea. I am only here for the summer. This is a temporary appointment at the institute. I don't want to give her the wrong impression."

"Seems to be a lot of that going around," Risa murmured, and Ben leaned in.

"What's that?"

She smiled. "Oh, nothing. Just talking to myself." She looked around at the art pieces. "I'm no good at shopping. I have no idea what to get. What if he hates what I choose?"

"Gifts should be welcome, no matter what. Especially ones that are obviously being chosen so carefully."

Risa hadn't thought of it that way before, but she liked the sentiment. They stood in front of a painting that featured a darkly painted salt marsh with a low, yellow moon hanging over the water.

"It's expensive—I don't know what kind of art would suit him."

"Hasn't Daniel suggested a gift?"

"He told me nothing was necessary, but I don't feel right going empty-handed."

Ben simply grunted in an agreeable fashion, and Risa continued to look, though she didn't plan on buying anything in the shop. They perused the pictures and sculptures slowly, discussing the elements of each as they went.

Ben was interesting, friendly. Even though he was extremely handsome, he didn't set off the firestorm of desires she felt around Daniel. It was nice, she decided, as she left the shop, being able to relax around a man. She could say she knew two of her neighbors now. She was catching on to normal life quite nicely.

"Would you like to join me for lunch, Risa, and then we can look at the shops on the other side of the street?"

"Oh, I don't think so. I'll just keep shopping, but it was nice of you to offer."

She started to turn away, but he stopped her. His touch on her elbow was just slightly insistent, and she drew back and he dropped his hand.

"I'm sorry. Please. I wish you would join me. I've only been here a short while, and I don't know many people outside of the lab. It's nice to be able to recognize a friendly face, and someone who knows the area so much better than I do."

"I've only been here a little longer than you—you moved in two weeks after I did."

His eyebrows shot up. "Really? I didn't realize that. Where do you come from originally?"

"You know, maybe I will join you for a quick bite." Risa smiled, hoping to deflect the question.

"Excellent!"

They walked the short distance to a quaint sidewalk café set off by a wrought-iron fence. The sun dappled down through the budding trees around them, and already there was a noticeable warming during the afternoons from just a few days ago.

Ben ordered drinks—Risa made sure she stuck with something strictly nonalcoholic—and she studied the menu. It occurred to her that this was her second meal in a restaurant, with a man, in as many days. Daniel had taken her to a small seafood restaurant that he knew well the night before. They'd eaten while he shared some details about his family, what it was like growing up on the Cape, though he didn't say any more about Stewart. End of story, he had said after his brief explanation, but Risa wasn't buying it—there was much more to that story.

She could see that Daniel's loss remained painful. She could relate. From what she gathered, he not only lost his brother, but his entire family, when he'd left.

Risa knew what that was like, to feel that loss. Her parents' deaths had created a gap in her life that had never quite healed. She'd filled it with work and duty, pushing herself as hard as Dr. Laslow wanted, and harder. When it had all ended, she thought that gap would swallow her.

Was that how Daniel was feeling? Did he use his job to avoid the pain of losing his brother and leaving his family behind? Was he afraid that if he weren't on a mission, putting his life on the line, that his pain would take him over and leave nothing behind? The sense of connection she felt to him strengthened. It was as if he were inside of her, filling her, but it wasn't physical.

"Risa?"

She looked over at him, embarrassed, although there was no way Ben could have known her private thoughts.

"I'm sorry, what did you say?"

"I was wondering where you came from before you moved here? Do you work here?"

Crap—she'd dropped her guard and now she was faced again with questions she didn't want to answer. She stuck to her old story.

"I used to live in D.C. I'm a writer—freelance."

"I would think a freelance writer would want to live in the city."

"I did, but things were…complicated. I needed to go somewhere, start new. I can do most of my work over the net. I can live anywhere." She was relieved to be able to tell truths that didn't reveal much.

"I see. And I assume Daniel was part of that complication, from what Kristy has told me?"

Her panicked expression must have spoken for her— what exactly did Kristy tell him and how much? Ben chuckled, waving at her with a careless flip of his hand as their lunches arrived.

"Don't worry, no deep female secrets were shared, but she did tell me Daniel had come here to make his feelings known—which I'd say he was doing quite well that night at the bar. And now you are going to a family party...so it appears his efforts have been successful?"

"It's really rather personal. I'm not comfortable discussing it, if you don't mind."

"It just seems strange that a man like that—he seems to be a bold man, not someone to stay in the background— would have had a hard time telling you how he felt."

"I told you, it was complicated." She felt some kind of invisible pressure, and didn't know why Ben was pursuing this avenue so aggressively.

"I would just urge you to be careful. There is a German saying: *Nachts sind alle katzen grau.*"

"All cats look gray in the dark," she blurted. Everything looks alike in the shadows; one thing cannot be told from another. What did Ben mean? How did that relate to Daniel? The mood between them shifted, and she felt antsy, ready to leave.

"You speak German?"

"Just a little. Picked it up from work."

"Of course. I'm sorry to make you uncomfortable. I won't press the point; however, if you don't mind me saying so, if Daniel hadn't shown up that night, I may have tried to charm you myself. Perhaps I am just jealous. I have a weakness for petite redheads."

Risa's spine stiffened. "Thanks for lunch, and the company. I really have to go." She stood and stepped away from the table to emphasize her point.

When he started to stand, as well, she put a hand out to stop him. "No, no—you stay. Finish your lunch.

Maybe Daniel's right, I don't need a gift. I'll pick up a bottle of wine later. That will do."

Something flickered in Ben's eyes, though nothing on the surface suggested he was being anything but gracious and accommodating as he nodded and sat back down.

"I'm sorry if I upset you. I hope you'll take my interest as a compliment. I meant no harm."

"I'm not offended. I just really have to go."

"Take care, Risa."

"I will."

DANIEL ARRIVED on Risa's doorstep at precisely six o'clock, his sister's warnings of showing up at seven sharp still ringing in his ears. He supposed if he was going to see his family for the first time in almost a decade, he should be on time. He just prayed they'd had the mercy to warn his father. Daniel had spent the day working, avoiding the apprehension about seeing his family by drowning himself in research, but in the end he'd given up and went to buy a gift.

He didn't shop around long, and settled on a pricey bottle of Scotch. It wasn't the most personal gift a son could buy for his father, but then again, he had no idea what his father would want from him, if anything. And if the elder MacAlister decided to give the Scotch back to him, Daniel mused, it might come in handy by the end of the evening. Give a gift you'd buy for yourself; isn't that what the etiquette gurus said?

He was so caught up in his thoughts he barely noticed the door opening, until Risa appeared. The knots in his stomach wrapped into a tight curl of arousal. She only made brief, fluttering eye contact, turning quickly to lock the door behind her—she was nervous, too. His eyes moved over the curves revealed by her fitted white dress, her narrow shoulders covered by a diaphanous blue shawl that had his fingers itching to remove it, making the satin skin underneath accessible. But seduction was part of his plan; he intended to ease her into it, to treat her like a beautiful woman should be treated, so that she would never settle for less. It had the side effect of doubling and tripling his own desire, as well.

"You look incredible. That dress…"

She stepped back, smoothing her hands down the front and screwing her lips into a grimace. "Are you sure it's not too much for a family party? It was one of Kristy's picks, I had no idea—"

He stepped closer, swallowing deeply, unable to hide the desire in his voice. "It's perfect, but who cares what anyone else thinks? I can't wait to get out of there and get my hands on you. In fact, I don't think I can wait…" He lifted the edge of the shawl and slid one fingertip along her shoulder.

"Stop it, Daniel. We have to go. Anna said seven."

Her tone censured him, but her eyes sparkled. She was pleased that he liked how she looked, her nerves disappearing—his, too. Suddenly he felt lighter. Maybe this wouldn't be so bad with Risa at his side. If nothing else, every time he looked at her it would distract him.

Now that they had decided to become lovers, even under the strange circumstances of their attachment, he was finding the slow path he'd decided on a torturous choice. He wanted her out of that dress—now. The shawl slid a little farther, and she tugged it back into position. But he wasn't done; his eyes refused to stop taking her in.

"Are you wearing makeup?"

Her porcelain cheeks turned bright pink, and it made him ache—how was he ever going to get through this evening without embarrassing himself?

"Just a little—Kristy did it. I told her to go light."

"It's just right…though you're stunning without it." Her cheeks turned even warmer—he was having an unexpected degree of fun. He hadn't felt quite this way since he was young, teasing his girlfriends in the same playful way, though he meant every word.

She turned, walking away from him down the hall. He followed, smiling at her discomfort at the compliments—he planned to offer more, so she'd just have to get used to it.

When he held the door of his rental car open for her to get in, and her dress rode up, exposing a length of bare thigh that was a sculptor's image of perfection, he nearly groaned out loud. What had he gotten himself into?

As he crossed to his side of the car, the only thing he was sure of was that she wasn't guilty of any treason against her government—his research confirmed that. He couldn't find anything questionable in Kristy Kelly's background, either, though Ben Richter was a little cloudier, but apparently aboveboard.

So now his only objective was making sure Risa

adjusted to real life well enough to erase any future threat of her drawing the wrong kind of attention to herself—though he wasn't sure if the attention *he* wanted to show her was exactly the right kind.

"Are you okay? Nervous?"

He started the car, looking at her. "Why?"

"You're being quiet in a really loud way right now."

Reaching over while the car was still in Park, he took her hand and placed it over his crotch, where he was still hard from looking at her and thinking about how it would be to settle in between those perfect thighs that had tempted him just moments before.

"I'm just a little tense—but not from thinking about the party. That dress is killing me."

She looked surprised, but didn't remove her hand. In fact, she squeezed lightly, as if testing his reaction. He thought about shutting the car off and dragging her into the backseat. But not now—not for her first time. He'd maintain some kind of control if it killed him.

He hadn't expected to feel this much need, this crazy desire. After his last assignment he'd had some fun, some R & R in D.C.; the women he dated knew the score. He took them out, they had a great time, they had great sex. Enough, he thought, to take the edge off of a long stint of abstinence. Or so he'd thought.

Not even close. Risa took her hand away, and said, "I can go change into jeans if it's a problem. You can't have *that* happening all night around your family."

Pulling her hand up to his lips, he closed his eyes, exhaling deeply, reaching for patience. "It won't matter what you wear—I'll be imagining you out of it. So, let's go, and get this over with so we can leave and make that happen."

The way she looked at him nearly did him in: pure feminine pleasure was written into every delicate feature. Though Risa was a virgin, her seductive instincts were sharp—she was enjoying this. Good. He turned back to the wheel. He meant to make sure she did enjoy herself—that they both did. And then he'd leave and put it all behind him. But not until he got Risa Remington out of his bloodstream.

"How far away is it?"

"Not quite an hour. I'm glad you decided to attend."

"You're right—it's good to meet people. I'm getting better with it. And I wanted to be with you."

Her simple statement warmed him, maybe much more than it should have.

"I'm glad. I think you'll like them, too. It will be fun, don't worry."

His words were meant for himself, as well as for her. The sunset behind him dimmed as he drove along the coastal highway. Finally, they turned into a long, winding drive and parked beside the other cars in front of a huge, shaker-shingled house.

"It's a gorgeous house," Risa observed.

"It was a good place to grow up—a nice neighborhood. Nothing seems to have changed much. Of course, my father bought a good deal of the surrounding land to make sure it wasn't swallowed up by development. He likes his privacy."

"Is your family rich?"

Daniel smiled at the bald question—he enjoyed the fact that Risa said what she thought, not bothering to mask her questions in the coy politeness and innuendo most people did.

"No, but land was cheaper back then, and they worked hard to pay off the mortgage. It was a challenge with five of us around. Both of my parents worked hard all of their lives, and are enjoying the fruits of that now."

From the noise filtering out to meet them, he assumed the party was being held out on the back patio and yard. It was a nice evening. The perfect time to have a gathering outdoors, before the mosquitoes and other bugs took over the woods behind the house.

Still, he felt trepidation set in and slow his steps as he approached the house. Maybe he shouldn't have done this—it could be a horrible mistake, for all of them. The instincts that served him in his work, the ones that called "flee!" were resounding in his mind, and were hard to resist.

He jumped when he felt Risa's fingers entwine with his. She looked up at him, catching his gaze and holding it. All he could see was her.

"It'll be fine. Press the bell, Daniel."

He did press the bell, though it felt ridiculous. He'd walked through this front door for two decades of his life—with his siblings, after school, with friends—and now he was ringing the bell. Like a guest. A stranger. When the door opened, and his mother appeared, he couldn't speak at first, and grasped Risa's hand a little tighter. Apparently, his mom didn't know what to say, either. When she wrapped him in a tight hug, he let out the breath he'd been holding.

Risa released Daniel's hand, stepping back and letting him enjoy the moment with his mother. Watching them, she had to look away as her eyes started to sting, thinking about how long it had been since her own mother had held her just like that. Of course, she'd been very small at the time, but she could see the love in Daniel's mother's expression, and remembered how it had been.

Dorothy MacAlister was a small woman with a flaming red mane of hair. Daniel had mentioned it was his father's sixty-second birthday party, but the woman he was married to didn't look anywhere near that age. She gazed at Daniel as if she'd found gold.

Risa was also fascinated with the emotion so evident on Daniel's face. The two exchanged greetings in low tones, and then both turned their attention to her. She started to back up one more step, but was quickly caught in a hug just as Daniel had been. Staring over the older woman's shoulder, she glanced at Daniel for help, patting the other woman loosely on the back, and hoping she would be let go sometime in this century.

Daniel just smiled and shrugged.

When his mother released her, she stood back, sizing up Risa in such a way that she felt like squirming, but then Daniel's mother smiled and nodded as if she were satisfied.

"You're just perfect, dear. Just as Anna described you. I don't think I have seen a prettier girl ever, but don't tell my daughters that." She took Risa by the elbow, hooked Daniel with the other—Mrs. MacAlister had some smooth moves for a mom—and escorted them in the door, chattering all the way.

"So, how long have you two been a couple? You do look striking together... Daniel, set those gifts on the table there, with the others... Everyone is out back. You should join them, but I want you to myself for a moment. Risa, you and Daniel worked together? And he let you go?" She looked at her son as if he had lost his mind. "But at least he had the sense to come back after you." She waved away Risa's attempt to speak and kept going. "Oh, Anna told us everything about the incident in the store—very romantic, I'd say. And it brought him back to us, too—fate, on every level, I believe."

Risa found herself smiling. Daniel's mother was not what she would have expected, and it made her curious about his father. And Daniel himself. Her discomfort was evaporating, and she turned to see where Daniel was. He stood on the other side of the room, staring at pictures on the mantel of the huge stone fireplace.

Dorothy noticed, too, and glanced at Risa, worry dimming the happiness in her eyes. But she took Risa by the elbow, walking with her to stand beside Daniel. Risa noticed the pictures of two younger versions of the man beside her—Daniel and Stewart, she assumed.

They stood in the grass of the large yard, arms slung around each other, laughing, holding a football. Daniel looked so young, impossibly handsome and without a care in the world. Why had he decided to live his life in the shadows? How had he become so serious, and so feared?

"There are my two handsome boys, Risa. Has Daniel told you about Stewart?"

Risa wasn't sure what to say. "A little."

"We still miss him every day, but life goes on. The best part is how the stories come back—you may lose someone, but they never really go away if you keep them in your life with stories. It was hard to talk about for a while, but it gets easier. Twin boys were a challenge, I'll tell you—they gave us a run for our money, didn't you, Daniel?"

He sighed, and Risa watched him stare at another picture, one of his mother and father—and she could suddenly see where Daniel got his looks from. His father was bigger, blockier, but the same handsome features were evident.

"We should go. Give Dad our best, Mom, or better yet, tell him I didn't show up." Daniel stepped back, heading for the front door. Startled by the suddenness of his move, Risa stood in place for a moment. But before Daniel's hand could reach the doorknob, his mother's voice stopped him cold.

"You had better not set one hand on that doorknob, Daniel Lewis McAlister."

Daniel met his mother's gaze, his chin set solidly. Risa wanted to help, but she wouldn't have known in a million years what to do.

"He won't want me here, Mom."

Dorothy McAlister crossed the room and took her son's hands in hers.

"Daniel, he's lived for your return, whether you believe that or not. You need him, too—I can see it. You're both cut from the same stubborn, stupid cloth, and you've denied each other peace for ten years—don't you think it's time? We lost one son, Daniel. When you walked out, we lost two. But now you're back—go see your father." She looked at him sternly, leaning in, but Risa could still overhear. "Don't be such a wuss. It won't impress your girlfriend."

Daniel shook his head in resignation, but when he lifted it, he was smiling, albeit tensely.

"Okay, Mom. I'll try. For you." He looked at Risa. "Ready?"

"Sure." As she joined them on the way to the back patio, she was anything but.

8

DANIEL HUNG AROUND the edges of the yard, counting the minutes until this would be over. He'd greeted his father, who'd met him with a gruff "welcome back," and a firm handshake before moving on to his other guests. Arthur had a much warmer greeting for Risa, who was making a hit with everyone—she'd been ensconced in conversation with Anna and his other sister Lisa for over an hour.

She was doing well; he'd stayed for *her*, he told himself, letting her enjoy the party and get to know his family. She could depend on them if she needed help after he was gone. The idea was like a lead weight in his gut. He could tell by the knowing looks and the veiled comments that everyone thought he was here to stay. They believed Risa would be the anchor keeping this particular ship in harbor.

It triggered his misgivings yet again, about what he was doing here and why. The rationalizations he'd formed to slake his desire for Risa shattered around him. He'd cleared her of suspicion, at least in his mind, and she seemed to be adapting just fine. She didn't need him—and he didn't need her.

He certainly shouldn't make love to her, knowing he

was going to be leaving. As much as she said she understood, she really had no idea. He should leave her alone, let her life progress naturally, let her share her body with a man who would stay.

However, the unfair truth was that he wanted her. As selfish as it was, he wouldn't leave her for someone else. A woman's first lover was memorable, for better or worse—and Daniel wanted to be with her forever, in her memories, at least.

Standing by the stone wall, listening to the laughter that rang around the yard, he'd never felt so separate, so distant. He didn't belong here. He was tempted to jump the stone wall and disappear into the woods, but he never was one to take the coward's way out.

"You look like a man with the devil coming up close on his backside."

He turned to find his older brother Alan joining him and breaking his solitude. He was surprised. Alan had always been a little separate, born six years before the rest of them. Their mother always said it was supposed to be two—Alan and one more—but then when the twins came, and she had three boys, she had to keep trying to get some more women in the house. She'd done it, too. Anna and Lisa came shortly after.

However, Alan was more like an only child, graduating into the next level of school ahead of them, always set apart. He had older friends, different interests and was halfway through college when Stewart and Daniel had barely hit high school. It didn't make for a close relationship.

"Something like that. How are you, Alan?"

"Good. Busy."

"Are you still running the best restaurants in Boston?"

His brother looked at him speculatively. "No one told you? I've been out of restaurant management for a year now—my bank account was doing fine, but my blood pressure wasn't. It's a hornet's nest, the restaurant business."

"You seemed to thrive on it, from what I remember."

"Times change. People, too. I took what I knew and I'm planning to open my own hotel. Small, luxury accommodations. Someone else can do the day-to-day management."

"I'm impressed. When do you break ground?"

"Late summer. We've bought the land, up in Brewster, and we're working with the architects now. We should be ready to open next season."

"Exciting news. I'm sorry I haven't kept up."

His brother looked at him speculatively. "Frankly, I wasn't sure we'd see you again, Dan. I'm surprised all it took to bring you back here after so long was a beautiful woman, though I will say, she's a hit. Mom is thinking about wedding invitations already. You know, unless Anna decides to use her maiden name, you're Dad's only hope for an heir to carry on the name for the MacAlister clan."

"What about you? No special woman in your life?"

Alan looked away, then turned a level gaze in his direction. "I guess you really are out of the loop. There is someone special. We've been together about three years. His name is Steven."

Daniel digested that bit of information smoothly, surprised again, but not shocked. "You're gay?"

"As the sky is blue."

"Are you happy?"

"Yes. Immeasurably."

"That's great." Daniel tipped his drink in his brother's direction and cast a look around the yard. "Is Steven here?"

Alan grunted. "Hardly—you could say Dad is not exactly supportive. He'll put up with it as long as I come around alone, and don't 'act gay,' as he states it."

Daniel shook his head. Looking at his burly, well-dressed brother, he couldn't imagine a person less likely to "act gay." Alan was about as far from the flaming gay stereotype as could be imagined. But as there was no malice in Alan's tone, Daniel smiled, offering, "Not the most open-minded man, our father."

"That's an understatement. Though he does seem to like Risa. Probably because she's got that red hair, like Mom."

"I hadn't really made that connection. It's not that kind of thing."

"Oh. What kind of thing is it?"

"Temporary."

His brother nodded. "I see. Didn't sound that way. I caught word you came all the way here after her. That doesn't smack of 'temporary.'"

"I came here to…make things right. We parted on bad terms back in D.C." He never dropped his gaze from Alan's, speaking convincingly. The lies fell off his tongue so easily he was almost ashamed after his brother's honest confession. That was the thing about leading the life he'd had—lies became commonplace, even the ones you told yourself. He rarely felt bad about it, as he did just then.

"Ah. So you'll be leaving soon, then?"

"I think so. Yes."

"Just for the record, regardless of what the old man says, what happened with Stewart wasn't your fault. He was an adult—he made his own choices. We all do, for better or worse."

"I guess that's the bottom line. But I influenced his choice—and his choice left him dead."

"It was still his choice. You've paid for it enough."

Daniel turned to fully face his brother. "Why are you bringing this up with me now?"

"It's good to see you. I know we weren't always close, but in recent years, I've been a bit of an outcast myself. As your older brother, though, I guess I felt there were things I could have done, should have said—"

"It wouldn't have changed anything."

"Things can always change, Dan. It's the way life goes. And we can change them, too."

"Thanks for saying so."

Alan laughed as he held his hand out to his brother. "A man of few words. You're different, Daniel. You used to be more lighthearted."

Daniel shook his brother's hand, shrugging when he let go. "Like you said, people change."

He didn't get to elaborate as he heard a cry from across the yard and veered his attention from the conversation to see everyone rushing to where Risa had fallen to the grass, unconscious.

RISA STOOD BESIDE Agent Daniel MacAlister, the two of them close but not touching—touching was strictly forbidden—as they huddled behind a rock in the cold climate of the Nevada desert. She cast him a sidelong look, tempted to lose her balance and brush up against the hard-looking man just once. What would she see in his mind if she did? Was there a chance he might have some small awareness of her hidden somewhere behind those dark eyes? She wouldn't do it, though—the implications were too dangerous, for both of them, if they breeched protocol.

It was pitch-black and they checked their equipment, making sure everything worked, exchanging brief whispers and sharing a curt nod before they both began their mission: to break into the secret lab that had been discovered beneath the desert. U.S. intelligence knew there were terrorists in the country—that knowledge was almost commonplace since 9/11. Only recently discovered, this lab was well hidden. If the tip they'd received was correct, whatever was happening here was big. They were to stage a surprise attack before any information could be erased or hidden. Hopefully, intel discovered here could shed light on other operations happening on U.S. soil.

Satellite imaging had displayed the bulk of the building sprawled out under the desert, camouflaged by the crumpled structure of a long-deserted airplane hangar. Sand, scrubby vegetation and animals had over-taken the nearly buried remains of the old building, nearly making it part of the natural landscape. Only someone who knew what was hiding down below would even bother with a second glance. The heat, the difficult landscape and the cover made it a perfect hiding spot for enemies within the country. But not for much longer.

Daniel turned toward her. "We're set. Let's go. We'll move in first, you hang back. We'll let you know when it's clear."

She nodded, but inside she fought the frisson of agitation that niggled when she was told to stay back, with other agents running the show, taking the lead. *She* was the one with the superpowers, *she* had strength enough to handle the biggest, toughest adversary they could send her way, but it would never happen. Her job was to come in after and sift through the computers and the minds of the people they'd found. She was just a tool they used, not a real agent; the thought rankled more than usual of late. The teams she worked with didn't know her; they thought she was a freak. She'd earned their fear, but not their respect, nor their friendship. She wanted more, wanted to be more, do more.

Dr. Laslow always told her she was too valuable to risk, that she had to remain separate from the others for her good and for theirs. Maybe, if she was so valuable, they'd have to start seeing things her way for a change, she pondered. Maybe she could start making some demands of her own.

"Remington. Snap out of it and keep up."

Agent MacAlister's sharp, cold voice shook her out of her thoughts as they converged on the entrance to the hangar. They walked into the dark space slowly, night-vision eyewear allowing them to see their path. Agent MacAlister found the hidden panel in the floor where they would be able to enter through a duct system that supplied fresh air underground. The space was narrow, and there were other entrances, but this one had shown the least chance of detection by the lab's security or human presence.

MacAlister went first, then his men, one staying back to flank Risa. They all kept a healthy distance as she moved down into the opening of the floor. She tried not to feel the slight—these men were a team, a unit. And she wasn't part of that.

Her duties had always been clear, and she accepted them, but as she detected Agent MacAlister's scent in the closed passageway, she found herself losing her concentration again. She'd never been so distracted on a mission—and the few times she had, it had always been when she worked with Daniel MacAlister.

As her feet landed on the floor below, she scanned her surroundings. It was a high-tech facility, more so than she expected. Machines hummed in a low throb around them, and the air was cool, the light dim. MacAlister gestured "this way" and they moved swiftly, but silently, after him.

She watched as fighting broke out, chaos surrounding them in a flare of fire and smoke, the sounds of one human being overcoming another one. Though she hadn't received the go-ahead, she saw her target clear and free—the computer at the core of the lab, protected by a glass chamber. She made a decision—the computers could be damaged in the fight, and information would be lost. The team was meeting more resistance than they'd counted on—she had to do her part as quickly as possible.

Sliding along the wall through the open door to the central area of the lab, she crouched, trying to stay out of sight. Laying her hands on the controls, she let her mind drift into the system, connecting with it and becoming part of it—for the time she'd maintain the link, she was part of the system and it was part of her. They were physically, as well as mentally, connected.

Then something happened, but everything blurred—she'd seen something, but she couldn't make out exactly what it was. She was trembling, fighting to maintain the connection as something vibrated all around her, shaking her to the core.

Blinding light screamed through her mind and she screamed with it; there was pain, but it all felt distant as she was overcome with the sensation of falling backward, falling for a long time. Everything was dark, blurry. Her head was hurting so badly she couldn't think—what had happened? Had she been shot? Was she dying?

The only thing she could see was MacAlister's face over hers, his strong arms hoisting her up over his shoulder…his voice asking her what happened. But she didn't know. She tried to speak, but she couldn't seem to make a sound.

DANIEL WATCHED Risa where she lay on the old twin bed in the room he'd shared with Stewart growing up; everything else was different. His mother had made a guest room of it, but the bed was still the same. Well, except for now there was only one bed, not two, as there had been back then.

Risa lay on the remaining one, pale and unconscious though obviously under some kind of stress, and he was helpless to reach her. He didn't like feeling helpless, ever. But wherever she'd gone in her mind, she was inaccessible to him. He'd tried everything: he'd shaken her, shouted at her and—even though he'd felt embarrassed about it—kissed her. Like he was freakin' Prince Charming coming to her rescue, except that he'd failed.

She was still out cold, her skin clammy, her pulse unsteady. He feared she might need medical help, and was tempted to contact Jack. They couldn't risk using a regular hospital until they knew what was causing these episodes, and if it were somehow related to her losing her powers—or getting them back.

He hadn't considered that—could it be her abilities were trying to reassert themselves, and were causing her some kind of mental trauma? Was that even possible? The reports he'd read stated her brain had basically been fried by the electromagnetic pulse that had been set off in the lab—and all of her abilities were rooted in her nervous system. They were gone for good. The headaches and passing out were simply side effects, but should have been gone by now. Instead, they seemed to be getting worse. She whimpered, and he clenched his jaw, wishing he could pull her out of whatever memories were causing her pain, if that were even the case.

He'd managed to get her upstairs, claiming she had low blood sugar, and reassured everyone that she'd be fine in just a few minutes. But what if she weren't? His family wasn't a group to be put off easily.

He didn't hear the door open behind them and startled—taken by surprise twice in a day. It was just his mother, but it could have been anyone. His instincts were shot, and he hated it.

"How is she? Should we call Dr. Price?"

"I think she'll be okay. If not, we have a doctor who works specifically with agents. She'll see him. I can have a plane ready with a phone call if it's necessary."

"Is this something work related? Did she quit work for the government because she was ill?"

He knew his mother was perceptive, but she was unknowingly tripping far too close to the truth. Still, there was no way to deny it.

"Yes, but don't worry—it's not fatal, or contagious."

His mom laid a hand on his shoulder, and he almost flinched. But she left her hand there, her voice calm. "I wasn't worried about us, dear. I'm worried about Risa."

"She'll be okay," he said with more conviction than he felt.

"You care for her." It was a statement, not a question, and he chose not to respond. His mother sighed, removing her hand. "You stay here with her, and let me know if there's anything we can do to help—anything at all."

The surprise at her backing off must have shown in

his face, because she smiled as she looked down at him, where he sat on the side of the bed.

"I know she's in capable hands, Daniel. You'll know what to do."

With that vote of confidence, his mother slipped out of the room as quietly as she'd come in. Daniel didn't know what he'd done to deserve her confidence, but it was a relief to know she wasn't going to push the situation.

Risa didn't look as if she'd be waking anytime soon. Scooting up on the bed beside her, he took her pulse—it was getting stronger. She had some color in her cheeks, and seemed to be breathing more easily. Maybe the worst had passed. Either way, he'd stay right here until she awoke, and they knew she was okay.

Then he was going to have a talk with Jack White about what the hell was going on.

"DANIEL?"

His name fell unbidden from Risa's lips as she awoke, searching unfamiliar surroundings with a quick snap of alarm before realizing he was right beside her. She looked down—he was sleeping, his hand wrapped around hers. It was curiously intimate, even sweet, in a way she never would have expected.

Maybe more so because she had been caught up in the distant echo of her memory, confirming what she'd been told but hadn't remembered: that Daniel had been the one to pull her out of the lab explosion. She'd awakened with the sense of his arms around her, and wondered if it were part of the memory, or a reflection of the reality she was sharing with him now?

Staring down at their fingers woven together, she closed her eyes and tried to picture anything that might come—as it had so easily before. But the touch only triggered her memory of what had happened between them the day before, and her awakening hunger for more. She had lost her ability to walk inside people's minds, but she was gaining something else—an entire array of emotions and sensations that had been denied her for all that time. She was eager to explore them.

Shifting beside Daniel, she leaned in, inhaling his scent and letting his masculine presence surround her as she laid her head on his shoulder, careful not to wake him. Extricating her hand from his, she placed it on his flat stomach, enjoying the warmth he radiated through his cotton shirt. She explored the finely tuned pectoral muscles of his chest, hard even while he was relaxed, and then moved over his shoulder and down over the smooth curve of his bicep. Every touch created a new memory in her mind; everything about this was new. Her heartbeat thudded in her head, her entire being reverberating with the thrill of being free to touch a man in this way.

"I guess you're feeling better."

His words caused her to pull back sharply, but he captured her in one sleek move and kept her hand splayed on his chest over his heart, which beat steady and strong under her palm. She looked up, and saw his eyes were still closed, but there was no doubt he was fully awake. She wondered if he had been the entire time she'd been touching him.

"I feel fine. It was another episode."

"I figured. Do you want to talk about it?"

She propped up on one elbow, bringing herself more or less even with his gaze, his eyes now open and not sleepy at all.

"I was remembering the mission where we broke into the Nevada lab—the explosion, and you, carrying me out."

His eyebrow shot up. "You can remember that? You were stone-cold out at the time."

"I guess there were a few minutes before I lapsed into the coma where I could sense your presence. I saw your face, felt your touch."

His gaze became much more guarded at her last revelation. "You remembered me touching you?"

She nodded, knowing what he feared. "I couldn't sense anything—I was already fried at that point."

What might she have seen if she'd been able to read Daniel? It suddenly hit her as an opportunity lost. He wasn't exactly the most communicative man she'd ever met, and deep inside she wondered how he felt about her, what he thought about her, what his secrets were. Not the state secrets, nothing to do with his job—she probably knew a lot of that, anyway. No, she wondered about the secrets of his heart, and if she would ever be allowed to know them.

"We should go."

He was already lifting up, separating from her. The space between them felt cool, and she supressed a small dash of hurt; for a few minutes, she'd felt closer to him than she had to anyone since her parents died. But she schooled her expression into practiced neutrality and slid off the bed, joining him.

"I hope I didn't cause any concern for your family."

"Of course they were concerned. But I managed to cover for you, and they knew to let well enough alone."

"I should come by another time and apologize for ruining your father's party." The hurt she'd felt when he moved away from her emerged in her voice, but he obviously thought she was just worried about his family, and he turned to face her, his voice reassuring.

"They'd love that. You really bonded with them quickly, especially Anna and Lisa. I'm sure they would love to see you, but don't feel the need to apologize. You couldn't help what happened."

The warmth of his words soothed some of her feelings, and she smiled. They crept out of the house, and moments later were zooming down the deserted coastal highway, everything quiet and dark in the middle of the night.

"May we stop?" she asked, after awhile.

"Here?"

"There was a parking area a ways back. I've never walked on the beach at night. I'd like to do that, if you aren't too tired."

"I'm more worried about you. You should get home, lay down."

"Daniel, I'm fine. These spells seem to get more severe, but they don't appear to have lingering effects.

But it did make me antsy. I've been sleeping for hours. I want to walk."

He pulled the car to a stop in a small parking lot near the guardrail. "Okay. A walk it is."

She shucked her shoes and drew her shawl more tightly around her. The sand and the air were cool, though not uncomfortably so. She decided to attempt the conversation again.

"Not to bring up a sore topic, but your sisters told me a little about Stewart, and what happened. It sounds like your brother's death was just an accident. Why did it stop you from going home for so long?"

He stopped walking, shoved his hands into his pockets and stared out at the expanse of darkness before them. A few lights signaled the presence of boats, but other than that, the watery world was black. It made her feel small and sucked up into the moment, as if nothing else existed around them.

"Stewart might have been my twin, but he wasn't inclined toward any kind of agency work. The only reason he went was because I did. Some misplaced sibling competitiveness—I was never sure why." Daniel shrugged, turning to walk along the surf. "I didn't discourage him, even though I knew the underwater dives were tough for him—he'd almost drowned as a child. He panicked and I should have stepped in and stopped him from going down."

Risa could hear the raw edge of pain still evident in his words. "So you blamed yourself even before your father did."

"He never approved of Stewart going off with me."

"You both quit school to go?"

"Yes. The corporate life wasn't for me—Dad always said he wanted us all to live easier lives than he did, but he never really took into consideration what we wanted. Stew would have been a great lawyer, though. If he'd lived, if I'd stepped in and told him to get out. To go back to school."

"Would he have listened?"

"I could have tried harder. Should have."

"I understand, Daniel, but your family doesn't blame you, so maybe you shouldn't blame yourself, either." She stepped forward, sliding her hands around his middle, stopping his progress down the beach and hugging him close. She jumped slightly when a cold wave slid up the sand and licked at her heel. "Oh, I didn't realize we were that close to the edge."

"It's hard to see out here in the dark. Cloudy. No moon."

His hands were large and warm on her back, steadying her as they stood silently in the dark. Risa knew he wouldn't talk about his brother anymore, and she knew she probably hadn't changed his mind. Wounds that deep weren't so easily healed.

"Thanks, Risa. But I'm supposed to be the one helping you get back to normal life. I'm not sure I ever could have one again. Or want one, for that matter."

She sensed the subtle warning of his words, as well as their literal meaning, and looked into his face, even though she could barely make out his features in the dark.

"I'm not asking for anything, Daniel. But I think they deserve a little something more from you."

"I've caused them enough suffering. If nothing else, I remind them of what they lost."

"And if you leave them again, you'll cause them more."

"Suddenly you're the expert? There really isn't any choice. It's who I am, what I do."

"Daniel—"

"Listen, I don't want to talk about this anymore. Not when there are better things we could be doing."

She barely had time to open her mouth and object when he descended, taking her lips in a hard, insistent kiss and cutting off any arguments. In the back of her mind, she wanted to push him away and finish what she'd been about to say, but the warmth of his skin, and his mouth, combined with the chill of the air and the water on her feet had her senses swimming. His touch was getting addictive, and within moments she was clinging to him and kissing him back with all the passion she had bottled up inside.

She anchored her fingers in his hair, and his arms were like a vise around her. They were pressed so close together not even a whisper of air could move between them as they consumed each other, their soft sighs and moans mingling with the sounds of surf around them.

Risa followed Daniel's lead as his cupped her backside and lifted up; she wrapped her legs around his hips while not giving up his mouth for so much as a second. He handled her shape and weight as if she were nothing at all, growling in approval as he moved her against him intimately. He was hard again, and the delicious friction he was causing between her thighs had her moaning in delight, seeking more.

Daniel could barely retain a rational thought, and this was going to be over much sooner than he wanted it to be if she kept moving against him like she was. Risa was seducing him—he'd thought it was supposed to be the other way around, but he wasn't complaining. He was so hard he ached, and she was irresistible, not that he wanted to resist.

They would be lovers. Whatever came later, he pushed it back, out of his mind. He was here now. As he explored the cool, silky skin of her throat with his lips, his thoughts flipped for a moment to their lack of birth control, but on the heels of that notion he remembered that Risa was sterile; it appeared the accident had taken the privilege of having children from her, too. A sliver of sadness hit him but he let it go as he continued to pursue the goal of learning every inch of Risa's firm body.

Her skin was cool. He explored the slopes and valleys like a blind man, committing each touch to memory. She shivered when his hands unerringly moving over the globes of her incredibly smooth derriere, slipping his fingers under her dress and between her cheeks to find the thin thread of satin that pulled a groan deep from inside of him. He slipped his hand underneath, winding it around the length of his fingers, and tugged the sweep of material tight, hearing her gasp against his neck.

"Daniel…"

"How did you know I love thongs, Risa? That slice

of material disappearing down into places I want to find, to explore…it just tempts me even more…."

"I wanted to tempt you. I didn't know if you'd like it. But I'm glad that you do." She cried out again as he tugged, showing her how much he liked it, and making sure she liked it, too.

"I love it, but it has to come off now. I want you naked."

He didn't give her a chance to respond, but pulled the strip of material carefully away from her sensitive skin so as not to hurt, and with one deft move, ripped it clean and dropped it to the sand. Moments later, the dress was gone, as well, and he almost died with pleasure when, completely naked, she purred against him, rubbing the tight, shapely length of her slim form against him.

"Slow down, sweetheart. This time, we have all night."

Kneeling in the sand, he was level with her flat stomach and started there, dipping his tongue into her naval while running his hands over the lean muscle of her legs. She dug her fingers into his hair, and she pulled tight when he nipped the delicate skin at the top of her thigh, but it felt good—everything with Risa felt good.

Licking his way along the crevice of hip and thigh, he lingered there, littering kisses over her skin as his hand found familiar territory between her legs. She was slick and hot, as turned on as he was, and he murmured thanks against her skin.

Gently opening her, he smiled at her gasping response as he pulled his fingers along the path her soft folds created. His own needs flared as she cried out and bowed toward him, her body a hot invitation for him to do whatever he wanted. He tried to remember this was all new to her—or mostly—but it was difficult when her responses were so bold.

"Risa, I want to taste you…."

"Please, Daniel…I want everything you can do to me. I want to feel everything that's possible to feel."

Her words floated down to him on feminine pants of breath that excited him further. He planned to satisfy her desires with enthusiastic thoroughness. Daniel had a reputation as a ruthless man, a man who pursued what he was after, and rarely failed in his mission. With Risa, he didn't want to be ruthless, though his pursuit of every pleasure he could find for both of them would be.

He moved her legs apart more widely, letting her settle and balance as he left hot kisses along the curly patch of soft hair that blanketed her secrets, allowing her to get used to the feel of his mouth in this new place, but only for a moment.

Parting her soft lips that held the delicious pearl within, he found it with his tongue and felt her shuddering response, licked again, tasting her more insistently. He slid one hand down the back of her delectable ass, nesting his fingers inside of her, moving gently until she screamed with pleasure and he felt her inner muscles confirm what he'd been trying to accomplish—her total and absolute pleasure. She was uninhibited and unafraid, and it turned him on as he'd never been before.

But as much as she might be cavalier about sex hurting the first time, he knew it very well might be unpleasant, and he wanted to give her as much satisfaction as he could, make her as ready as possible, before he took their coupling to its conclusion.

"You like this, sweetheart?"

"Oh, yes, Daniel…but I want more…I want you this time. Please."

He wasn't about to disappoint. Rising, he pulled the erect tip of one breast into his mouth, and suckled its sweetness while his hands continued their journey, rubbing and wringing one more lovely orgasm from her body as she nearly buckled. He caught her, though, saving her from the sand.

As she cuddled into him, he felt a surge of warmth, the same need to protect he'd felt earlier, and he nearly backed off again, protecting her from himself—until her hand unerringly found his erection, rubbing him in just the right way. She whispered what she wanted so blatantly he lost all sense of apprehension.

"Undress me, Risa." It was a husky command, and she was more than willing, pushing the shirt up over his head eagerly, and shocking him when she drew a nipple between her lips while she undid his pants. Her feminine instincts were right on; somehow, while unpracticed, she knew just how he liked to be touched. He couldn't hold back the sharp groan of pleasure that ripped through him, the cool air barely cooling the intense heat of his body. It was time; he couldn't wait anymore.

Wrapping her in his arms for a long, deep kiss, he hoisted her up and loved how she enfolded him with her legs, the slippery evidence of her desire against his sex.

She instinctively sought him, but he slowed her down, getting the position right, easing himself inside just a little bit, letting her get used to his size, giving her body a chance to accommodate his.

"Oh, Daniel, it feels so good…I need this. I want all of you…please. *Now.*"

She pushed against him, insisting, and it caused the desire to roar through him. As much as he intended to stay in control, he found himself thrusting forward to meet her, biting his own lip to hold back the scorch of pure sensation that assaulted him as the snug fist of her body closed around his shaft, making him dizzy with the sheer intensity of it. He stilled, planted deep inside of her. He could barely catch his breath to speak clearly.

"Risa, are you all right? Tell me—we can stop."

Though stopping could very well kill him on the spot, he would. But he felt the brush of her hair against his cheek as she shook her head in the negative and kissed him, moving tentatively, then more boldly, and inviting him to do the same.

He was determined to last for her, but the way she was moving against him was almost too much. She was wild, returning his thrusts with such complete lack of control it was infectious, crying out her pleasure and urging him on. He gave in, letting loose, restraint a distant memory.

Digging his fingers into the tender skin of her bottom, he chased down his own release, her body holding his captive as she came with another thrilling cry as he hammered into her, milking him, sending him over the brink. He capitulated, the searing explosion throbbing through his entire body and pouring into hers.

Breathing heavily, he didn't realize how tightly he held her to him until she wiggled, still catching her own breath. Their skin was slick, and the air started to chill them; he felt her shiver, and held her closer.

"Risa, are you okay?"

Too late, the worry assaulted him. He'd been too rough, too out of control with her inexperienced body. But no sooner did the recriminating thoughts occur than her sexy chuckle erased them.

"Okay? You want to know if I'm *okay?* Hmm…"

He could hear the shiver in her voice and let her go to pick up her dress, shaking the sand out and handing it to her. She grabbed the material, and his hand with it, making him listen, her voice more exuberant than he'd ever heard it.

"I'm absolutely breathless, Daniel. This is the most alive I have ever felt, the most free, the most… incredible. I don't know if I've ever really felt anything until now—or tasted, or touched, or saw. So yeah, you could say I'm okay. A little sore, but even that feels good. You make everything feel good."

He almost laughed at her dramatic hyperbole, but the male animal in him soaked it up. All of the emotions her words brought forth started burgeoning, because, well… she'd made him feel alive, too. Like he could breathe. And feel, and taste. And he wanted her again, as well. As soon as humanly possible. Risa wouldn't be sleeping alone tonight.

But he didn't say so, not with words anyway. She slipped her dress on, and he moved behind her, nestling his cheek over the tresses that covered her ear—another part he had yet to explore—and placed his jacket over her shoulders. He was hard again, wanting her again, and moved against her behind to let her know. She pressed back and had him catching his breath, thinking about lifting her dress and taking her again, right now, from behind, until they were both lost again. He pushed the desire back, his voice hoarse with it as he spoke.

"I think we lost your new shawl."

"I'd call it a fair trade." She turned to him, taking his face in her hands. He still couldn't see her clearly, but he was moved by the sincerity in her voice.

"Thank you, Daniel—if I died right this minute, that was the most amazing experience I could ever imagine."

"Risa…" Her words weighed in his gut, replacing some of the lightness he'd felt, and he didn't want to think about it. Not right now.

"Hmm?"

"Let's get back to your place."

He felt her smile against his shoulder. "I was hoping you'd say that."

9

RISA CAUGHT A VIEW of herself in the new mirror Daniel was hanging right now in her entryway—it was a beautiful antique they'd found at a Sunday flea market. Just looking at the delicately sculpted pewter frame made her immeasurably happy. Looking at the man hanging it up figured in, as well. It'd been two weeks since they'd made love on the beach, and she felt like a new person— she'd teased him that she'd been "reborn" but that wasn't far from the truth.

"Those highlights are kickin', but let's get this bookcase put down and you can come back and admire yourself later," Kristy teased at her over the top of the three-shelf case they'd just found on yet another shopping binge. Risa was coming to enjoy shopping very much, especially now that she had some idea of what her "style" was. Kristy had been right in her first observations about Risa's apartment. Risa had never really paid much attention to objects, to decorating, either herself or her surroundings. But now she couldn't seem to stop.

She'd started with a new haircut and blond highlights in her copper hair. Kristy said it made her look like she'd spent all day at the beach. From there, Kristy and Daniel had both helped her make myriad changes in her life. She was recreating herself for the first time, and she loved it. She discovered she loved muted, earthy colors and plants. She'd already filled an entire window with plants in bloom, and she enjoyed taking painstaking care of them. The gardening books she'd collected in just the last few days would fill one level of the bookcase.

She loved old, beautiful pieces of furniture, like the mirror, and the gorgeous depression-era glass lamp that Ben was currently bringing in behind them. The modern pieces she'd looked at felt too stark to her, and her life had always been stark. She felt as if she were coming a little more alive each day.

She was learning how to drive, and had started looking for jobs. The money she'd earned working for the government and never used over her lifetime would hold her for a while, but she needed something to do, a purpose in life. She had no idea what that would be, but at least she wasn't afraid anymore. She'd accepted that, while one phase of her life was over, a new one was beginning.

She cast another look in Daniel's direction as he appeared to be testing the strength of the hooks for the heavy mirror. Everything was because of him. Kristy had become a good, enthusiastic friend who was proving to be a huge source of support, but the deeper changes, the willingness to risk and to explore, were all because of Daniel.

He'd changed her life in every way, in more ways than he'd ever know, inside and out. She felt her eyes fill, and shook herself out of her thoughts—she still didn't like showing overt emotion in front of others, and maybe she never would. Looking around, she rolled her eyes at Kristy and Ben, who were sneaking a cuddle and a kiss near the kitchen.

"Hey, you two, cut it out. Time to get the sofa and the chair—all hands on deck."

"You're such a slave driver," Kristy sighed, disentangling herself from Ben's arms.

"It's just these last two pieces. I'll owe you breakfast at Betsy's tomorrow, as promised."

Kristy groaned appreciatively. Betsy's was a local fifties-style diner where the motto "eat heavy" was taken seriously.

"Lead on, boss. Nothing like the promise of apple-filled pancakes as motivation!"

Risa turned her smile toward Ben. "You, too. You didn't have to pitch in, but we sure appreciate it."

Ben smiled, but seemed hardly able to take his eyes off of Kristy. Risa was happy for the couple. Things seemed to be moving along nicely for them, and it made her think about what it would be like if she and Daniel didn't have so many secrets between them. Though she'd thrown herself headfirst—and heart first—into her affair with him, she reminded herself regularly that's all it was. Daniel would be leaving soon. As soon as she was solidly on her feet, he'd disappear from her world as completely as he'd entered it.

"Are you okay?" Daniel came up close by her side, his lips brushing the lobe of her ear with a kiss as he whispered the question, and she couldn't stall the racing of her heart. She couldn't seem to stem any of her reactions to him, which was still disconcerting, but she enjoyed the sensations and the emotional experience so much.

"Fine, just a little tired from hauling everything."

"Why don't you sit—three of us will be more than enough to get the rest."

"Thanks." She turned her head, kissing him and darting her tongue out for a taste. He captured it with a groan and pulled her closer, deepening the kiss until she pulled away with a gasp, choking on a small laugh.

"Not now. Let's get the couch up here first."

Daniel's dark eyes flared at the suggestiveness in her voice. "Sounds like a plan."

They hurried through the rest of the move—Risa couldn't wait to be alone with Daniel and was pleased to see that Ben and Kristy were just as eager to get back to Ben's place. The four agreed to meet for breakfast before Risa closed the door, turning to face where Daniel stood beside the older-style Stickley sofa and chair she'd bought at an auction. They were pieces she never could have afforded otherwise, and the rich, deep upholstery and sturdy Mission frame beckoned her. She sauntered up to Daniel, feeling flirty and confident.

"Want to test out how sturdy this construction really is?"

He didn't waste time talking—Daniel was, if anything, a man of action. The laughter that bubbled up inside her was smothered by his mouth as he captured her lips in a scorching kiss, his hands moving over her with practiced familiarity. After two weeks of frequent lovemaking, she felt as if he'd shown her every kind of pleasure a man and woman could share—but each time he still managed to surprise her.

This time, she wanted to surprise him. Hating to separate herself from his devouring kisses even for a second, she did, murmuring against his lips, "Daniel, I'm hungry."

"Me, too, sweetheart…starving for you."

"Daniel I want to make love to *you* this time."

It took him a second before her words seemed to soak in, and she wasn't sure how he would react. Daniel was used to being in control, and most of the time that worked very nicely for her, too. But she wanted to make him the focus of her attention like he'd been doing for her since they'd become lovers. She wanted him at her mercy in the wonderful ways she'd been at his. He studied her face, and nodded, looking a bit apprehensive.

"What did you have in mind?"

She stood a few feet in front of him, and took a fortifying breath. Never dropping his gaze, she started removing her clothing one piece at a time, dropping it to the floor around her, testing to see what turned him on or what didn't. His eyes were burning with desire as he watched her, the evidence of his arousal clear in his lap. He groaned and clenched his fists when she experimented by touching herself, letting her fingers wander casually over her breasts, and lower.

"Take your clothes off for me, Daniel."

He did so, quickly and eagerly, his chest expanding

and contracting in deep breaths as he sat back, squeezing a hand around his fully erect shaft while he continued to watch her watch him.

She approached slowly, dipping a finger into the well between her thighs, then trailing it around the edges of his lips before she took his mouth in a heart-stopping kiss. He groaned, grunting an objection when she drew away, but then murmuring his approval as she kissed her way along his chest, across his stomach, finally closing her mouth over his length, licking upward to the head in one heated swipe.

Gratified as she watched his fingers dig into the edges of the cushion, his body bowing up, she did it again, sucking the pearl of moisture that emerged from the tip of his penis, enjoying his flavor immensely. Energy zinged through her, and she felt it pulse back and forth between them.

"Risa, don't stop…suck me. Hard," he panted.

"My pleasure, darling," she purred the endearment, feeling the connection between them deepen. It was the first time he'd given himself over to her like this, and the first time she'd been brave enough to risk using one of the endearments lovers shared. Though he seemed to do so casually, it was a meaningful moment for her. She poured all of the emotion she was feeling into making love to him, giving him as much as she was taking.

She ran her hands over him wherever she could reach, lifting up over him as she gloried in the vision of male ecstasy laid before her. She dragged her tongue over the flat, lightly haired planes of his stomach, stopping to lick one dark, flat nipple. Deftly, she maneuvered into position and enveloped him inside of her body with one quick, hard thrust downward. She knew that, although he could be tender and soft with her, he liked it best hard and fast, and she planned to give him everything he wanted.

His guttural cry and the way he gripped her hips as he drove up inside of her drew an equally jubilant exclamation from her lips as she balanced and squeezed him between her thighs, finding just the right position and riding him without inhibition. In only seconds, she reached a screaming climax, but didn't relent even as his body clenched in racking spasms of release.

She wasn't finished with him, and it appeared he was okay with that. Amazingly, he still surged hard inside of her. Pushing him back in the sofa, she scooted forward, blanketing him with her body. She sought and found his cock and took him inside again, rotating her hips in a slow, indolent move that had his heart pounding under her cheek, every part of them pressed together.

She whispered her thoughts to him, erotic secrets, and he answered, their breathless voices mingling in a chant that accompanied their rhythm as she continued to move against him, demanding more. She'd never felt so deeply connected to anyone.

The world seemed to blur around her, the contact between them, inside and out, becoming her universe, and she sighed into his neck. She never wanted it to end. One orgasm surged through her, starting at the center and moving to each part of her like ripples over water.

She heard her mellow moan echoing the pleasure almost as if she were hearing it secondhand, as if it came from some outside source rather than herself.

Everything felt different…she was sinking in pleasure, lost in Daniel, giving herself over completely to the magic that was being woven between them. She felt comfort, as well as passion, trust, desire, and…something else, some deep emotion that tugged at her heart, but which she wasn't ready to admit yet.

In the way his hands moved over her and the things he whispered in her ear, she felt it emanating from him, too. The desire, but also something…more. The universe consisted of only the two of them, but as the world closed in around them, her body continued to move even as her mind went to a different place.

She'd merged with him in more ways than one, and yet more orgasms broke between them until she realized what was happening. Their whispers mingled, the words hot and pulled from the depths of desire, wrapping around them, but she was no longer speaking her own words.

She was speaking his.

Their chant was spoken in perfect unison, their language perfectly metered. Somehow, his thoughts, his voice, had become one with hers. She knew what he was feeling, thinking, saying…

She tried to pull back, realizing it as he crested again, and she cried out with him, feeling the pleasure zing through her body from his, every element of their mind and body connected. Only then, when he heard her, and realized what had happened, did he let go, pushing her away, his eyes blazing with shock, his chest heaving.

"What the hell?" Daniel's voice, though still ragged with spent passion, shouted the question at her as he pushed her roughly up by the shoulders. She couldn't concentrate, the break so jolting that her mind seemed to short-circuit for a second. When her vision cleared, she looked down into his eyes, which were filled with outrage and betrayal.

"How did you do that? How, Risa? How'd you get in my head?"

She was trembling from head to toe, a late afternoon breeze wafting in the window and sending a chill over her feverish body. She and Daniel weren't joined anymore—in any sense of the word—and she suddenly felt exposed, confused and frightened. She shook her head at him, feeling horrified at what had happened, at what he must think, and scrambled backward, seeking her clothes, unable to look at him even as he grabbed her wrist and yanked her forward.

"Oh, no you don't. You're not going anywhere. I want to know what happened. Have your powers returned? Did they ever really go?" His brow scrunched as he seemed to think back, remembering. "When I caught you in my room, holding my hand, concentrating—you were trying to read me, weren't you? Tell me the truth, Risa. Now."

Her heart broke at his words, realizing how damning that other innocent moment was, and she moved away, dragging her shirt and jeans with her, though all she could do was hold them in front of her. Her body was spent and her knees barely able to hold her weight. She couldn't make sense of what happened anymore than he could.

He yanked his pants on, his expression feral. He'd become the dangerous, lethal man she'd always known. Gone was the friend, the tender lover. A shiver of fear shuddered through her as he stared down coldly.

"You're going to tell me what's happening, Risa. One way or the other."

She shook her head, still blurry, pain kicking in. What had happened? "It—it isn't what you think. I don't know why it happened…." The words emerged on a hoarse whisper; it was an effort even to speak. Daniel's presence became secondary. She was exhausted and confused, and the pain was taking over again. She pulled her shirt on as well as she could and tried to stand, but she stumbled and fell, landing on her knee, hitting something sharp. She didn't even hear Daniel call out to her. By the time he reached for her, everything turned dark.

"You know what you need to do, Daniel. This sounds like a critical breach." Jack's voice was a thread of steel on the phone, and Daniel closed his eyes, finding it difficult to say the words.

"I wouldn't go that far. I don't even know if it was a single event or something more serious."

"Carry out your orders, agent."

Daniel resisted—he was a trained agent, not a lapdog. He had to make life-and-death decisions all the time, and he wasn't about to take a life if he wasn't sure.

"I'm planning to find out more first."

"You're going to interrogate her?"

Daniel's gut clenched. "That's the plan."

"Fine. Find out who she's working with, what she knows, and then take care of the problem. The more you find out, the more damage we can contain. She has to know about Laslow's disappearance—there's no one else who would have known about that lab, where to find him."

"And if I find out she's not guilty of anything?"

Jack was silent, and Daniel knew his older, more experienced superior could detect the thread of hope in his voice that Daniel had tried to mask. But Jack knew.

"You got in too deep, didn't you? You fell for her?"

"I can do my job. I'm just trying to be thorough."

Daniel knew that Jack didn't buy it and spat out a curse under his breath.

"I'll be counting on that, Daniel. Whatever happens, whatever the fallout from this is, it's not just on her head—it'll be on yours, too."

The line went dead, and Daniel knew he'd made a critical mistake. Jack would call in backup; it was standard procedure when they thought they had an agent unable to carry out orders. And Daniel could very well become a target, as well, unless he found a way to either save face and deal with Risa, or clear her name.

All of his devils were swirling to life in the darkness of the room as Daniel watched Risa, handcuffed to the bed, still unconscious. He didn't trust her, but he didn't trust anyone else with her. It was a unique situation, to say the least. Now the stakes had risen for both of them.

Before she'd blacked out, she'd said something about him being wrong—he wanted to believe that. He didn't know how he could be wrong. He knew what he'd heard. She'd been reciting his thoughts just as they rose to the surface of his mind, speaking every word right along with him. The evidence was damning. She'd been in his head, there was no denying that.

What troubled him was that she'd seemed as shocked by it as he was. She could have been faking, knowing she'd slipped up in a weak moment. But it created doubt enough for him to want to wait until he was absolutely sure. But letting Jack sense that doubt was a fatal error.

Dr. Laslow had been kidnapped, snatched out of his secret lab—the emphasis on *secret*. Few people knew the location or the way into that lab. Risa was one of those who did. As convincined as he'd been in her innocence, the evidence was mounting in the other direction.

The process of checking and calling in all the potentially exposed agents had already begun; projects would be stalled, everything grinding to a halt until they could assess the damage.

Even though she'd pried open his head and looked inside, he couldn't really imagine hurting her. He'd crossed a forbidden line, letting himself not only get involved with, but also actually falling for, his target. Now what?

There were too many questions, none of which could be answered until she came to. He eyed the small pack on the nightstand. It held a syringe of sodium thiopental— an anesthetic used by most dentists, and an old-fashioned but effective and relatively harmless truth serum.

Although he knew it was his only option—Jack and his associates would do far worse if they had their way—the idea of interrogating Risa was painful. The heaviness in his chest made it difficult to breathe. Risa'd told him about being drugged by Laslow, and now she would experience the same thing from his hands. But getting the absolute truth from her could save her life— or seal her fate. Either way, he had to know. Then he would do what he had to do.

Watching her sleep so peacefully was killing him— from what he could tell, she wasn't suffering any flashbacks; she'd just passed out. When he looked at her, his body tightened in response, remembering the softness of her skin, the heated grip of her body. But his body hadn't been betrayed as his mind had been. Still... Daniel had never been particularly sentimental about sex, but he'd known long before today that what they had was more than that. He should have walked away after the first time.

"Daniel?"

He sat completely still as he watched her eyelids flutter, and she shifted, frowning when she felt the tug of the restraints. *Test one,* he thought—if she hadn't lost her powers, she could break those cuffs without even trying.

But she just tugged again, seeming confused, and then her eyes widened and became haunted as she lay back quietly on the bed—she was remembering. She wouldn't look at him, and it stung, in spite of everything.

"How are you feeling?"

"Does it matter?"

"Yes, actually."

Something in his tone must have set her off, and she turned her head to watch him warily as he grabbed a blood pressure cuff, and proceeded to check her out.

"Have you already called them?" Her voice was weary. He knew what she meant.

"Yes."

"So that's it, then? Do I get to defend myself at all? I didn't know that was going to happen. I don't know why—"

"Risa, stay calm, please. You're not helping."

It was the tone he'd mastered, the tone he'd used hundreds of times in interrogations—distant, neutral, almost placating. The conversational tone of someone who was in complete control, and who was about to do something relatively unpleasant. It was chilling, even to him, this time.

He could tell by the look in her eyes that she knew—she knew what he was about to do. The flicker of fear was quickly extinguished, but he'd seen it, and while he could understand it, he didn't want her to be afraid.

"It's only a little truth serum, Risa. A few questions."

She made no effort to break free. Instead, she looked him in the eye, her voice steady. "I guess I don't have much choice."

"Choice wasn't an issue when you got inside my head, was it? It was never a choice for any of the people you read, but did you ever think about how that felt to them?" He maintained the calm tone, though it was completely the opposite of how he was feeling inside, but he called on years of training to quell his emotions, and didn't look at her.

"I guess I didn't. I was working under orders—like you are now. Will I be waking up?"

He swallowed the clog in his throat and administered the drug with a steady hand while watching her eyes flutter shut. He didn't know if she heard his answer.

"It depends on what you have to say."

Within seconds, she was deeply under the drug. He asked a few questions—basic facts that would test the waters. He took a deep breath and got to the meat of the issue.

"Risa, have you been lying about having lost your powers in the accident?"

"No."

"So you have been living completely without your powers since you left the organization?"

"Yes."

"Was the accident part of a larger setup? Do you work for an enemy?"

"No. I would never do that." Her voice was breathy, but the conviction was strong, even in her drugged state.

"Have you used your powers to read any secret information from my mind, or anyone else's, recently?"

"No."

"How do you explain what happened when you read my thoughts earlier today?"

Her brow creased, and she stirred a little. The issue

clearly upset her. "I don't know. I don't know what happened."

"Can you explain to me what happened?" He pushed. She had to give him something. It was possible she could resist the drug, and he might have to up the dosage to overcome any inhibitions, though doing so was dangerous.

She stretched against the restraints, her body moving in a sinuous curve as she smiled, apparently remembering.

"We were making love. It was just so good, so amazing. I felt like we were so connected, I didn't want it to stop, how you were touching me everywhere, inside and out...."

She sighed in a way that brought the memories back for him and he went hard, cursing under his breath. He cut her off, lest she detail the entire event, which he wasn't sure he could stand.

"Yes, we were having sex. And then what?"

"I just felt like I...melted into you. Like we were connected, physically, but deeper, and I wanted more, wanted to let it happen."

"Let what happen?"

"Becoming one with you."

Daniel was stymied; so far, the only thing she sounded guilty of was passion. The notion sparked a thought—could the passion between them have somehow been responsible?

"Then what, Risa?"

"We were making love, whispering things to each

other. I didn't realize at first that my words were coming from your thoughts...and when I realized I was in your mind, I panicked, and tried to break away, but you were holding me so tightly, I couldn't."

He knew that much was true. He'd been caught up in the mindless pleasure of the moment, and he remembered how she'd pulled away for a second. He'd thought she was just shifting positions. He'd wanted her close to him, all over him, so he'd held her in place, and she'd come back against him—melted, as she described it— when he'd objected to her moving away. It had broken the spell between them just enough that he'd realized what was happening.

"Have you ever read me before?"

She frowned again. "I don't know. I don't think so, but I feel I can sense you better than other people."

"What do you mean?"

"Your moods, your wants. I can sense things, but not like I did before. I don't read them, I just have a...gut feeling."

"So this has never happened before?"

"No."

"Did you kidnap or help in the kidnapping of Dr. Laslow?"

The question, thrown out randomly, had her shaking her head resolutely. "No."

"Did you know about the kidnapping?"

"No."

He returned to the previous line of questioning, hoping that she really was telling him the truth.

"So you were able to read my mind because of the intensity of our physical connection?"

He found it astounding, but plausible. They had no idea what had happened to her mind in the accident, or how she came by her powers in the first place. Genetic defect was the hypothesis. The basis of her family's abilities seemed to be electrical. All human bodies carried electrical currents. Could it be possible that their intimate contact had somehow reconfigured the electrical impulses that allowed her to read thoughts, through no intention of her own? If that were true, then she was innocent.

"It was more that that…." she continued groggily, and he sharpened his attention.

"More?"

"Just before it happened, it was my emotions…they took over. The physical joining was more intense because of how I felt. I'd never felt that way before. It was strong. So very strong."

His brow furrowed, and he wasn't one hundred percent sure what she was trying to express; her sentences were a little jumbled, as if she didn't know how to explain it, either, which was perfectly reasonable in her state. The drug paralyzed higher cognitive functions, like reasoning and deceit, so she could only really answer basic questions, not analyze or argue. Still, he watched her try to get a grip on her own thoughts through the haze of the drug. When she spoke this time, her voice was confident, assured, and her words set him back several paces.

"I think it happened, that the connection was so deep, because I'm in love with you."

10

OPENING HER EYES SLOWLY, Risa took in her surroundings, recognizing Daniel's room. She blinked, testing her awareness, her mind clearing. Relief came first, then wariness. He'd drugged her—interrogated her. What had she said when she was under? It didn't matter—she had nothing to hide. She was free. And she was still breathing. Two good signs that he'd found out what he needed to know.

Then paranoia kicked in again—was this a trap? Was he waiting to see what she'd do?

She lay there, the muddled, shocked feeling replaced with an increasing burn of anger. Daniel was the first man—the first person—she'd truly trusted since her parents died. Though it wasn't wise, her feelings had skyrocketed past mere sexual chemistry.

But the first time something unexpected happened, he'd doubted her, pushed her away, restrained her and proceeded to interrogate her.

Did it really matter if what he found out quelled his suspicions? She'd let herself forget who he really was and what he was capable of. She'd left herself open to this. He'd just done what he was assigned to do, but did that have to include making her fall for him?

No, that wasn't fair—she'd lapsed into that particular stupidity all by herself. He'd been honest with her at the beginning, but she'd fallen into the trap of thinking maybe he'd changed. The man she'd fallen for didn't seem like the ruthless agent she'd known, but he was. He'd proved that by standing over her with a needle just a few hours ago and telling her maybe she'd wake up again, depending.

She wouldn't forget again. She'd probably never be able to forget. It was the most humiliating, frightening thing she'd experienced in her life. His taunting words haunted her as she'd dropped off and lost all control. She'd always felt what she'd done had been for the best of humanity, to help the good guys. But how could she know who the good guys were? Was Daniel a good guy? She'd never really questioned her work, she'd just done as she was told. The implications of that hit home painfully.

Her muscles felt weak, limp, but when the door creaked behind her and he appeared in the hall that led to the bathroom, she didn't care if she had no fighting skills, or if her superstrength was gone. Her anger and shame made her feel as if she had the strength of ten women. She jumped from the bed, vaulting toward him, kicking, hitting, scratching, screaming, hoping she could hurt him in some small way, not that it could compare to how he'd hurt her.

She took him by surprise and got a few licks in before he grabbed her and pinned her arms behind her back, bringing her front into close contact with his. When she tried to lift a knee, he anticipated and blocked, pushing her backward up against a wall, trapped, unable to move.

"I see you're awake."

"In more ways than one. Let me go, you *bastard!*" She hissed the curse through her teeth, struggling against him, but he simply held her until she wore herself out.

"Someone woke up on the wrong side of the bed— I guess I shouldn't have removed the cuffs."

"Yeah, you probably got off on that—an unconscious woman in cuffs."

He simply arched an eyebrow. "You're the one who violated *my* mind, if I recall. Took advantage of me in an unguarded moment."

"I tried to tell you it wasn't intentional."

"You'll have to forgive me if trust doesn't come that easily—how did you expect me to react?"

"You could have listened to me. You didn't have to, you didn't need to—" She wasn't able to stop the low, aching moan from escaping her lips. He'd taught her a lot over the past two weeks, and it seemed he'd provide her first lesson in heartbreak, as well.

"Risa, what's the matter? Are you ill? I didn't give you that much…"

The concern in his eyes was too much to take, and she bit her lip hard, pushing back the emotions.

"Why couldn't you just have listened? How could you think…how could you have done *that?*"

She couldn't finish, feeling her eyes sting with tears, and refused to lower herself one more iota by crying in front of him.

"I've done a lot of things in this job that people might

find unforgivable, Risa—things I'd never want my family to know about, which is part of the reason I stayed away. But doing that to you was maybe the only thing I won't be able to forgive myself for." His words shocked her into listening; she didn't fight or flee when he dropped his hold on her.

"You freaked me, Risa—seriously—when you got inside my head. It was too much. I couldn't deal with it."

"It wasn't on purpose," she repeated.

"I know that now. But I had to be sure. If there was the remote chance you were still…powerful, well, we had to know."

She noted his shift to *we.* "Still a company man first, hmm, Daniel? No matter what the cost?"

"You don't understand, Risa. Things have gotten much more complicated. We—I—had to make sure you weren't involved."

He was talking in riddles now, and she became impatient. "Involved in what?"

He watched her for a long moment. "Dr. Laslow was taken from his lab yesterday. They suspect he was kidnapped."

Her eyes widened, her mind making the connections within seconds. "They thought I was involved because of his work with me?"

"You know the lab, his habits. If your powers were still operational, then it added up to a rather unpleasant picture. I'm sorry I had to do what I did, Risa, but I'd do it again to make sure—for my country, and for you."

"For me? That's one hell of a rationalization."

"Maybe, but at least now I know you're innocent. I know you're telling the truth."

"And you couldn't have just asked me, trusted me?"

She saw the hard reality in his face, though he didn't respond. Of course he couldn't. She blew out a breath, running a hand through her tangled hair. "I guess not. I don't know how I managed to get inside your mind, Daniel, and I don't know anything about Laslow."

"I understand, but the agency is not so willing. They're convinced you're part of the problem. I tried to convince them to let me handle things, but I think I'm on borrowed time. I don't know how well I covered. You've become too high risk. Could be I have, too."

"You think they're sending others—to do what you couldn't?"

He nodded. "Things have been set in motion, Risa, but that doesn't mean we have to get caught under the wheels if we can act fast enough."

Something in his tone encouraged her, and softened the anger into something resembling hope; she took a step forward. What was done was done; everything between them had changed, but they had to focus on the present.

"Did you find out anything while I was under? Anything that explains why I was able to...do what I did?"

He hesitated, his jaw squared, a flicker of uncertainty in his expression. "The only thing that seems plausible is that there was something so complete about the physical connection between us in that particular moment that it led to some kind of momentary, involuntary mind meld. You said you tried to stop, but I wouldn't let you move, so I guess it was partly my fault."

Did he look somewhat regretful, or was it her imagination?

"I guess it's also possible your powers are reasserting themselves," he continued, "coming back, through no fault of your own. Maybe the accident didn't wipe them out completely? Maybe the damage was temporary. Have you had any other flashes?"

She shook her head, stunned with the idea. "No. But it's hard sometimes. I've started being able to sense things, like when Kristy is worried or when you are thinking about your family, even though you may not say anything. I thought it was just normal intuition kicking in. I never considered—"

She stopped short, considering his theory. She was just getting used to her "normal" life. What would she do if her powers returned? She wrapped her arms around her middle, fighting panic. A few weeks ago, that idea would have been a dream come true, but now all she could think about was everything she would lose if he were right, if her powers *were* coming back. What would she do?

"Hey, settle down…it's perfectly normal to have those kinds of insights about people you're close to."

"It is?"

"Absolutely. My mom and dad finish each other's sentences all the time, but they aren't mind readers. I'm just throwing out possibilities. I don't think we should jump the gun, but even if you did get them back, your grandfather and many of your relatives before him lived in the world with their powers, and did fine, right? You would, too. They couldn't make you go back."

She nodded, her mind racing ahead. "What else did you ask me? What else did I say?"

It was unsettling to have him poking around in her life, asking her questions she was induced to answer truthfully when she had no control, no memory. He could have asked her anything. She'd been completely exposed.

It struck her suddenly how awful it must have been for Daniel and for anyone else whose mind she had intruded upon, unintentional or not. She'd been raised to do what she did without doubt, but now she questioned her own actions. Everything was so confusing.

"I asked you a lot of the same stuff from different angles."

He looked away; she knew he was avoiding her, hiding something. Her intuition, it appeared, was operating again, and it made the difference clear. She could sense he was hiding something; she just didn't know what. But if he didn't want to tell her, did she have the right to push? She changed the subject.

"How do we convince them that I had nothing to do with Laslow's kidnapping, and what if whoever kidnapped him finds out about me? That's got to be why he was taken...someone knows. Or wants to."

Daniel nodded, looking relieved that they'd skipped the former subject of conversation.

"That's my thinking. The way we solve it is to find him, and that's what I plan to do."

She leveled a look in his direction. "You mean *we*."

"I mean, I. Alone. This is my job, Risa. Go somewhere no one will think of looking for you. Because Jack has already dispatched someone, I'm sure of it. We're not safe now. Not until we get this settled."

"No way. This is my fight, too. You can train me. You can show me what I need to know, and we'll do this together."

"We don't have that much time, Risa. Things are happening, we have to move."

"Then let's get started."

"Do I have to knock you out again?" He said it half-jokingly, but she wasn't sure about the other half of his intentions.

"If it means leaving me behind, yeah, probably."

They faced each other, the tension broken by the muffled ring of Risa's cell phone. She slid it out of her pocket carefully, peering at the number before answering.

"Kristy." She paused to look at Daniel. "Is this safe?"

"Don't take the chance. Get the number, turn it off and use the room phone."

She did as he instructed, and within seconds, had Kristy on the line. "Kristy, it's Risa."

Kristy was wound up, to put it mildly, and Risa spent a few seconds calming her down, her dread increasing as Kristy explained why she was calling. Risa covered the receiver, slanting a look to Daniel.

"She says she went to the store to get some things for dinner, and when she came back, Ben was gone. And she said she'd found a gun there a few nights ago, in his drawer. It's gone, too. No note. No sign of him."

It was a troubling coincidence, to say the least. After calming Kristy down and urging her not to say a word to anyone, Risa hung up, and filled Daniel in on the martial arts she'd seen Ben practicing, his level of expertise, the coincidental meeting and lunch they'd shared a few days before. Risa had had some "feelings" then about Ben, but she didn't know enough to trust them.

"I'd say this is a pretty large coincidence, given the circumstances."

"So what do we do now?"

He ran a hand over his face; he was tired, but she pushed her concern aside. She couldn't afford any more tender feelings toward Daniel. He'd said he couldn't trust her. He'd as much as admitted that, while it was difficult for him to do what he did, he'd still done it—he was still an agent, through and through. And he was keeping secrets from her. And that meant they had no future.

"I think Kristy is probably okay. But we need to get to Ben's and see what we can find. There could be something there that will lead us in the right direction."

"Let's go."

"Risa—"

"Don't waste time arguing, Daniel."

"I don't want you to get hurt."

She smiled sadly over her shoulder, headed for the door and slid under her breath, "Too late."

KRISTY WAS AT Ben's apartment when they arrived, visibly upset and curled up on the sofa. She jumped up, throwing her arms around Risa when they stepped through the door.

"Something horrible has happened to him, hasn't it? Otherwise you wouldn't be involved. Either of you."

She drew back, leveling a knowing glance at them both, and Daniel shifted uncomfortably, looking away. What Risa had told Kristy about herself was bad enough, but he wasn't about to share anything more.

"He could have had an emergency? Gone to the office?"

"I checked. No one has seen him. We were here, planning dinner, and he just disappeared. I was only gone for a little while. If he went, it wasn't work related. All of his files, his briefcase, his books—they're all here. But the gun is gone."

Kristy wasn't stupid. Still, Ben could be gone for any number of reasons, even though Daniel was sure he must be involved. It was what his gut told him, and he was usually right. Hopefully, if they looked around, they might be able to find something more solid to go on.

He walked away from the two women talking in low whispers. Never in his life had he had so much trouble staying on task during a mission. He was mucking this one up but good. Thanks to his lack of control, both his and Risa's life might be on the line. But God help him, all the way over, in the car, a knife twisted in his gut when she wouldn't look at him. She wouldn't talk to him unless it was necessary, and was careful not to so much as brush up against him when they walked side by side.

He wanted to fight, to have her angry and slapping at

him, whatever, he didn't care, as along as it meant she'd touch him. Even if she could read his every thought, he'd almost be okay with it—almost—except then she'd really see the truth. *I love you...*the words kept echoing in his mind. He didn't know what to do. Daniel had never loved a woman—not in the complete, emotional, soulful sense that he saw other couples share—but he'd never felt for anyone like he did for Risa.

Knowing she felt the same way couldn't help but draw him—if he hadn't killed her feelings with his distrust and drastic measures. But maybe that was for the best, in the long run. If he lived through this, if it all worked out, he'd go back to his work—it was what he knew. He wasn't cut out for the domestic life.

His cell phone rang, and he ignored it. They couldn't track him through it—a nifty little bit of technology kept that from being possible—and he didn't want to hear Jack White's voice right now. There was nothing he could tell them anyway.

"Do you see anything?" Risa's question was cool, businesslike, and Kristy stayed by the door, watching him with wary eyes. He turned to her; she might know more than she thought.

"Kristy, did he seem tense? Agitated at all? Was there anything strange you can think of in his behavior, his actions?"

He and Risa both moved around the front of the sofa at the same time, and came up face-to-face. Without so much as a flicker of an eye, she stepped to the side, taking a wide berth around. His fists curled in frustration as he resisted the urge to reach over and pull her up close, but he didn't really have any right to do that. Need, desire—but no right.

Kristy shook her head. "No, he was great. We had a great time, walked on the beach, got some dinner. He seemed very relaxed." Her eyes welled, and she swiped them quickly with the back of her hand, then stopped. "He did get a call before I left. I didn't stick around, though. It looked like it would take a while."

"Did he say who was calling?"

"No, and I didn't ask. Though you know, come to think of it, he never did say much. He'd talk a little bit about the work at the lab, but whenever I asked him personal questions, or things about his life in Germany, or anything like that, he'd answer vaguely, or turn the question back to me. I just figured he was shy about personal stuff. That was stupid, wasn't it? He's like you two, isn't he—but a bad guy?"

Risa had walked back around to where Kristy stood again, and placed a comforting hand on the woman's shoulder. She was getting much more used to casual touching, Daniel noticed.

"It's not your fault if he lied to you, or deceived you."

Daniel grew irritated, taking her words personally even if they weren't directed at him. He may have behaved like a dick, but he'd never lied. He'd been as upfront as possible with Risa. Blowing out a breath, he stemmed his annoyance, knowing she was just comforting her friend, not taking a dig at him. And he needed to concentrate. He needed to get information on that phone call, and find out who was on the other side—that could be their break.

His cell rang again, and he swore, yanking it out of his pocket. It was his mother—he just didn't need this. But his call record showed she'd been trying to contact him consistently, and so he gave in and pressed Talk.

He listened for a few minutes, then clicked it shut. Why did shit all happen at once?

"What now?" Risa asked, without rancor, but obviously able to read his mood.

His mouth tightened, and he shook his head. "Anna is in the hospital."

Risa was silent; how exactly did you respond to your CIA lover who'd just drugged and questioned you, but who was also clearly worried about his pregnant sister? All the signs were contrary, all the roads seemed to lead in different directions. Her emotions were such a mess all she could do was stare and say the first thing that came to mind, the simplest, most direct thing.

"What happened?"

"Her blood pressure was sky-high. She's being prepped for surgery, an emergency C-section."

"You need to be there." She crossed the room, but still maintained her distance. Every fiber of her being urged her to touch him, to comfort, to connect, but she couldn't. That kind of thing had no place in their relationship anymore. If her powers were coming back, or even if what he'd said was true and it was just something that had happened with him, because of their closeness, she couldn't risk it either way.

"I have to get a trace on that phone call." He switched his gaze from her to Kristy. "You should clear out—go back to Boston for a few days, stay with some friends or your family. Risa will call you when things are clear."

Kristy puffed up. "I can't do that! I have a job, responsibilities…and I know Ben wouldn't hurt me, no matter what he's involved in."

Daniel's voice was hard. "We can't be sure of that. We don't know who he's working with, or why—it's not safe for you until we know what's happening."

Kristy looked over at Risa. "I thought you said you weren't working for the government anymore?"

"I have to find out what's going on—they won't let me alone until we do. And I'd like you to be here for me when this is done—you're my friend, my *only* friend."

Risa took Kristy's hands in hers. "Please do as Daniel says. Take a few sick days—it won't be that long. I'll call you as soon as the coast is clear."

"But Ben—"

"We'll take care of it."

Kristy hesitated and then nodded mutely, turning to the door. "Okay. But you take care of yourself—you're my friend, too."

Risa smiled, relieved when the door finally shut behind Kristy. Then she turned to Daniel, who was looking at her with some strange expression. Admiration? She wasn't sure, but it made her feel like squirming.

"You handled that extremely well, Risa."

"I guess I just knew she wouldn't react well to being strong-armed."

"Good call. Now, I should be able to get those phone records within the hour, and we can keep searching here, though I doubt we'll find anything."

She looked at him in shock. "Daniel! Have you forgotten about Anna? You have to go to the hospital. Certainly no one will try anything there, and you have to be there for your family. How can you explain to them if you're not?"

His face was a neutral mask, and it made her want to hit him again, to make him show some emotion.

"You're going to the hospital, Daniel."

"Risa—"

"I mean it. You can run your traces or whatever from there—they'll probably even have computers you could use. It will give us time to regroup and come up with a plan, to find out more about Ben."

She was getting better at handling difficult situations, she realized with a sense of pride—she could see him relenting. Daniel clearly didn't like being on the receiving end of her orders, but it was important for him to do this. She'd felt the despair he still carried around because of his brother, and she wasn't going to allow him to use his job to hide from his family, or from the emotions he felt for them.

She only wished he felt as much for her. She was furious with him, upset, heartbroken, but she still loved him, and she wanted him to heal. Even if they couldn't be together, maybe when he left at least he would have eased some of the pain he carried around inside.

"Okay." He shook his head, as if in disbelief that she'd gotten him to agree. "But one hour, just to check on her and make sure she's okay, and we're out of there. We shouldn't stay in one place for too long."

She nodded resolutely. "One hour."

11

DANIEL NEVER FELT comfortable in hospitals, though he'd spent more time in them than he'd liked; it came with the job. There was happiness in hospitals, he knew, as well as sadness, fear, loneliness, excitement and joy. It was as if all the shades and colors of the human condition could be found within that one building. It was hard to know how to feel, what to expect, with private moments, painful moments, joyful moments unfolding along every hallway.

Following the painted line on the floor that led to the maternity unit, he turned his head away as they passed a doctor talking in low tones to a young woman who sank against her husband's shoulder while receiving the words. In another brightly decorated room they passed on the way, laughter and tears were shared with hugs.

There was so much *emotion* here; he wasn't used to it. In his life, emotions just got in the way. But had it always been that way? No. His childhood had been filled with laughter. Heaviness had only set in after Stewart's drowning; he'd never been able to forgive himself. Was everyone right? Had he been carrying that around for too long? His chest tightened as they walked to the desk and were cleared, a nurse emerging to take them to a waiting lounge.

"Waiting? I don't want to go to a lounge. I want to see my sister."

The nurse kept walking, moving efficiently along ahead of him, and shaking her head.

"You need to see the rest of your family, Mr. MacAlister. They'll bring you up-to-date."

It was taking a monumental effort for him to stay in control as they turned yet another corner. Images came unbidden to his mind; Anna being such a pest when she would bug him with his friends, wanting to join their fun; Anna struggling with geometry, and how he'd helped her for hours to pass a final; Anna's wedding picture on the fireplace mantel.

The nurse finally opened the door to a private room where his parents, his siblings...and a strange man he could only deduce was Steven, Alan's partner were. That was interesting, he thought idly. Brandon, Anna's husband, sat with their father, white as a sheet, and tense. They all looked pale, pinched and worried. They'd been surprised at his arrival, heads perking up, eyes expectant, and then shoulders slumping as if they'd been looking for someone else. He swallowed the lump in his throat. Of course they wouldn't have expected to see him walk through the door—why would they?

"Where's Anna? Is she okay? I want to see her."

They probably thought he had no place making demands, but he really didn't give a damn if anyone didn't like it. He wanted to know what was happening to his little sister—amazingly, all other thoughts about what was happening at the moment had evaporated. He hadn't even realized Risa was no longer by his side. Where was she?

"Anna's in surgery, Daniel. Come, sit down, we'll tell you what we know."

His mother had always been cool in a crisis—for all of her effusiveness, with five children she'd had to stand strong through a lot of emergency room visits and worse.

"Anna started suffering a lot of pain last night, feeling ill, and she thought she was heading into early labor— but she had an undetected uterine infection, and it became very serious very quickly. They're doing an emergency C-section."

"But she has two months left!" Of all the frightening things Daniel had witnessed without a blink, the idea of his little sister going into surgery terrified him. His mother patted his hand, her voice reassuring, though he could detect the thin ribbon of anxiety in her voice.

"She's at thirty-one weeks—that's very good. Babies at that point have a good chance of surviving. This is what they had to do to save them both, Daniel. It's very serious."

"What are you trying to say, Mom?"

"They just warned us that time is of the essence— they had to act quickly to save Anna and the baby."

He felt as if the wind had been completely knocked out of him. How many times had his sister called this past week and he'd avoided her? He knew she wanted him to make peace with his father, and he didn't want to talk about it. Now, he wondered if he'd ever talk to her again, and everything inside of him went numb, rejecting that thought. Anna *had* to get better.

"When will we know what's going on?"

"They assured us it won't be too long, barring complications. We just have to sit tight and wait. They were hopeful, Daniel, so we should be, too."

He heard her words, but didn't feel them. He couldn't just sit here and hope. He'd been trained to take action, solve problems; he did whatever was necessary, but he could always do something. However, sitting and fretting was beyond him; he just couldn't sit still. He'd have to do something while they were waiting for news.

"I have to go find Risa."

"She's here?"

"Yeah, but she must have decided to wait outside."

"Well, go get her, boy," his father's gruff voice interrupted them. "You don't leave the woman in your life waiting out in a hallway, especially at a time like this."

Daniel was shocked by his father's direct address; that brief admonishment was the most they'd spoken in years. He looked into his father's face somewhat quizzically.

"I'll go see if I can find her."

"You do that."

Daniel stood, sharing a few words with his brother and sisters, squeezing Brandon's shoulder silently before he left to find Risa. She wasn't waiting outside the door, and his heartbeat picked up, his mind darting back to the situation at hand. Risa was in real danger; she shouldn't be wandering around without him, even here.

It was unlikely anything would happen to them in the safe confines of the hospital, but it was better to stay close.

Luckily the attendant at the nursing station had been the one to give Risa directions to the small cafeteria down at the end of the hall. When Daniel spotted her sitting at a small table in front of a row of long, dark windows, munching on something, he approached her chair, glowering.

"Risa—are you *trying* to get killed?"

She glanced up at him, her eyes narrowing. "The food isn't that bad."

"You should have stayed with me, for one, and now you decide to sit in the most public place you can find, in front of a row of windows?"

She actually had the nerve to roll her eyes at him as she popped the last bit of a muffin into her mouth. "Daniel, these windows look out over nothing. Woods, water, marsh, a parking lot. No one even knows we're here—it's probably the last place anyone would expect."

"Yeah, and it's always a surprise when you get shot in the last place you expect." He ground the words out, unreasonably angry that she'd be so careless, and leaned down over her.

"Let's move away from this table, shall we?"

Though she hesitated, something in his voice compelled her to obey, and she stood, though her body language clearly expressed that she thought he was an idiot. Fine—as long as they were both alive, she could think whatever she liked. He was worried about Anna, and he needed Risa to be able to take care of herself for the moment.

"How's Anna? Did you see her?"

He shook his head, his thoughts and emotions volleying back and forth in a virtual ping-pong game of stress between the two crises he was managing just now.

"She had an infection, and they have to do a premature C-section to save them both."

Risa's belligerence melted, but she still kept her distance on the other side of the table they sat at, far from the windows. She hadn't so much as brushed up against him since the incident in the hotel room, not that he blamed her, but she was being almost too diligent about making sure they had no contact. Had he hurt her that badly, or was she afraid she might inadvertently "read" him again? He didn't really want to get into it, but he realized he missed the strength and the comfort of her touch. He wouldn't ask for it though—it was better this way.

"I'm so sorry—when will you know if they're okay?"

"Soon, unless there are complications, I guess the surgery doesn't take that long."

"You go—wait with your family. Why are you even here?"

"I came to find you—I noticed you'd slipped out before we went into the lounge. Why?"

She shrugged. "It was a family thing. I'm not family."

"Well—" he slanted a smile, unbelievably finding something humorous among all the worry "—I think my father won't let me back in that room unless I have you with me, so you'd better come along."

Her brow furrowed. "That's nice of them, but don't

you think it's better not to lead them on, make them think we're really a couple? You could tell them I just dropped you off, and left."

"I don't think they'd believe you would be that uncaring. I don't believe it, either. You're welcome with my family, Risa—we don't have to be a couple for that to be true. Like I said, they're good people for you to know when I leave."

She stood up, her posture stiff. "Yes, I know. Friends, contacts, people I could call if I needed something—do you ever stop thinking strategy, Daniel? Are there people you've had in your life who are just there, because you want them to be, or because you care about them, but not because they serve some sort of purpose?"

Her words dug, and he wanted to shout at her that she was one person he cared about far too much, and it seemed her only purpose was to drive him over the edge whether it was with desire or frustration.

"No, I don't stop thinking strategy, because that's what's going to keep us alive right now. Just because we're here doesn't mean everything else has gone away—there are people out there looking for you, for us. Dangerous people."

"People like you?"

"Yes, people exactly like me. It won't take them long to find out my family has had an emergency, and they'll track us here easily. We have to get out, lie low. We can't go back to the hotel or your apartment, and we shouldn't stay here longer than we have to."

"So where do we go?"

"I have contacts—I'll get on the phone and find a way off the Cape."

"To where?"

"I don't know yet. I need to make some calls, to get some information on Ben Richter—he's our only solid lead right now."

"How exactly are you going to do that here?"

"You go, sit with my family. Tell them...I don't know. Tell them something. I'll find a phone, make some calls, see what I can figure out. Come get me if anything regarding Anna changes. Can you do that?"

She nodded curtly, angling sideways ever so slightly as he held the door open for her so as to avoid contact, and it set his teeth on edge. If they weren't where they were under the current circumstances, he might be tempted to haul her up against the wall and remind her how good contact between them could feel.

As it was, he just followed her down the hall back toward the waiting room, and tried not to focus on how the sweep of copper hair brushed against the tender skin at the back of the base of her neck. He watched her progress, making sure she went into the room this time, and then doubled back, looking for a pay phone. Even though his cell was untraceable, he didn't want to risk Jack's team tracing them to the hospital any faster than they would eventually.

Like most black-ops agents, he had connections and contacts of his own that no one knew about—friends in powerful places who had gotten him out of tight spots when he needed them. He needed them now. It just so happened one of those people was a very wealthy Boston shipping magnate whose family had been kidnapped while abroad, and Daniel had been instrumental in saving their lives. The man had offered Daniel a blank check for whatever he needed, whenever he needed it—no questions asked—and he had the connections to get them off the Cape quickly and quietly. That would solve one problem.

The second problem was finding out what the hell was going on with Laslow and Richter. That was trickier, because he couldn't risk using anyone on the inside. There was no way he could get near a computer to hack his way around and try to find out, but he knew someone who could: Nolan Wagner, former boy genius and current techno-cop for the Hotwires, a computer crime team in Boston.

Daniel and Nolan had spent some time together in college, and while they were never exactly friends, he'd used Nolan's talents a few times over the years. Nolan was completely trustworthy. He would know how to handle anyone who came looking for Daniel. He was also a hacker of enormous talent, and if anyone could find out what was happening with Ben Richter, who he really was, and what was going on, Nolan could.

Daniel found the phone and started making his calls.

RISA FOUND Daniel attached to a pay phone not far from the nurses' station, and caught his attention. He hung up the phone, turned and practically sprinted back down the hall.

"They're out of surgery—they're going to be okay. Anna's in SICU, and the baby—a boy, by the way—is in the preemie unit. They're still not completely out of danger, receiving heavy antibiotics, but the doctors are optimistic."

Risa wanted to hug him when she saw the relief wash over him—it was so plain to see, how much he loved his sister, and how afraid he'd been, that she almost cried. Daniel had so much love inside of him, but he buried it deeply.

"We have to go."

Risa looked at him in complete disbelief. "You've got to be kidding! You are not going anywhere, Daniel MacAlister, until you see your new nephew. You can take a few minutes to do that, at least."

She knew he was about to argue, but the room had gone silent around them. He looked around to see everyone looking at him, particularly his father. The senior MacAlister seemed to be waiting for his estranged son to disappoint him—again.

Daniel took a deep breath, and to Risa's relief, made the right decision—no matter what was about to happen, Daniel needed this moment with his family.

"You're right." He looked at his father, who nodded in approval, and then at Brandon. "So, does my nephew have a name yet?"

The room seemed to relax at his question, and Risa found a spot to sit in the corner of the waiting room as the family all took their turns going to visit the new baby. She was tired, but happy for them, and glad that Daniel had stayed. He was obviously annoyed with her, sitting on the other side of the room, waiting until last to visit. When Dorothy MacAlister came into the room, her expression was tired and yet exuberant. She hugged them both, unable to contain the joy in her voice.

"He's just perfect, Daniel. Perfect. And they say we can probably see Anna by morning. She could be off the critical list soon."

"That's great, Mom. I'm glad everything turned out well."

Risa marveled at how he could sound so controlled, so much like a visitor, a guest, and not a part of the family who'd just gone through this harrowing, wondrous event. It infuriated her. She had no family; they'd been lost, taken from her, and she'd been raised by government officials and caretakers—a superhero who was essentially a ward of the state. She'd done what she had for so many years because it was not just her duty but her destiny, and because she had nothing else.

But Daniel did.

Daniel had this warm, incredible family, and he didn't have any inclination to be part of it. It was ironic—she was the one who was supposed to learn to live a normal life, but Daniel didn't want any part of his.

She didn't realize she'd phased out of the moment completely until his mother shook her shoulder a little. Dorothy looked down at Risa as Daniel left the room. "Risa, dear, would you like to see the baby?"

"They said only family…."

"I think we can make an exception. It's been so good of you to get Daniel here, and to make him stay." Risa started to object, but it was clear Daniel's mother wasn't under any illusions about her son's proclivities.

"I know he has something heavy on his mind, something serious. And I know what he does for his country—maybe not specifically, but I have some idea. He's not the first man in our family to make that kind of sacrifice. But I also know he's hurt—deeply—and he carries around burdens that aren't his to carry. I suspect you know that, too."

Risa, nodded, not really wanting to talk about Daniel behind his back, but curious about what Dorothy had to say.

"Daniel just has a lot on his mind right now."

Dorothy laughed, and her eyes sparkled as she took Risa's hands. "Very diplomatic, dear. It's good you can guard his secrets, though I think he has far too many of them. But what I know is that he listens to you—I've never seen anyone, except for me I suppose, tell Daniel what he was going to do in no uncertain terms and get away with it. No matter what's happening, it's clear he respects you, and my intuition tells me he probably has a lot more than respect for you."

Risa read the lilt in her voice, and started to object, but was cut off yet again.

"Don't worry dear, I'm not going to push the issue. I just hope whatever's between you two works out, that's all. I wanted to come back here so that Daniel could have his turn to go down and see the baby while his father is still there. It's time those two made peace. I always knew Daniel would come home. I had to believe that."

Risa smiled. "You set it up, to have them together in the room with that baby."

Mrs. MacAlister pretended to look affronted, but there was a quirk at the edge of her smile. "Mothers do not 'set people up,' dear—they just help them along a little now and then." She grinned, dropping Risa's hands and gesturing toward the door. "Now how about we go see my new grandson?"

Risa nodded, having the oddest feeling more had just transpired than she knew, but having absolutely no idea what it was. It felt nice, though, and she smiled as she followed the other woman down the hall to see the first baby she'd ever met up close.

"HE DOESN'T LOOK GOOD." Daniel hated to say it, but the impossibly small bundle of skin and bone wasn't what he'd expected. Everyone was so happy coming out of the ward that he was expecting more of a...baby. He hadn't seen too many infants in his lifetime, and his nephew didn't look well, hooked up to an impossible number of machines and seeming too small to handle it all. Arthur MacAlister shook his head, never taking his eyes off his grandchild.

"Of course he doesn't look good. He's sick, and early. He wasn't ready yet, but he's learned his first lesson in life—we aren't always ready for what comes our way."

Just as Daniel was feeling outraged at his father's

apparent insensitivity, the older man's voice softened with pride.

"But he's a MacAlister—oh, I know it's not his name, but it's his blood, and he's a fighter. We're all fighters, and this young one's going to be just fine."

"How can you sound so sure?" On one hand, Daniel felt surreal standing here having this conversation with his father, whom he hadn't said more than a sentence to in ten years, but it also felt incredibly normal. Right, even.

"Because I want little him to feel it—oh, now, I don't believe in all the hocus-pocus, but you can feel whether someone has faith in you or not, even a baby that small. If he knows we believe in him, it'll help."

"You really think so?"

"I do."

They were silent for a while, and Daniel stood looking down at the baby, trying to believe that everything would be all right—he wanted that for Anna so much he couldn't express it. Her baby was here in the world, and she didn't even know it yet. Daniel stood with his father as they looked through a glass window into the life-supporting box that held their newest family member. Arthur heaved a heavy sigh, speaking to Daniel though he never took his eyes from the baby.

"It's been too long, Daniel. I never intended to make it so you didn't come back. I was angry, mourning Stewart. If I said it was your fault, and I don't know if I said directly, but maybe in so many words, well, I was wrong to do that. I hope we've all paid enough for it."

Daniel blinked, not quite sure he'd heard correctly. "I beg your pardon?"

Arthur MacAlister stepped away from the glass wall, and met his eldest eye to eye. "I was destroyed when Stewart died, but it was his decision to follow you down there, his call to quit school with you to join up for that crazy-assed training, not yours. It was his decision to get in the water, even though he wasn't good in it. I knew that then, but I couldn't say it. I needed someone to pay, and I guess I laid all of that grief at your doorstep, son. You were always the stronger of the two of you, but I leaned on you too hard. A father shouldn't do that to a child."

"I don't know what to say, Dad."

And he really didn't know. He'd accepted the burden of guilt for Stewart's death, since he felt responsible whether or not his father thought he was. His father's blame had just been confirmation of what he already felt.

He knew his brother wasn't cut out for CIA training, and he'd been in the water with him that day. Stewart followed because he loved to be with Daniel, and they had a subtle competition, as brothers always do. When Daniel had resisted, had pushed Stewart to stay in school, Stewart had taken it as a slight. "I did try to talk him out of it. He wouldn't listen."

His father nodded. "Sounds about right. You were both hardheaded, but Stew always was more foolhardy. Probably makes you good at what you do."

Daniel couldn't fight the well of emotions burgeoning at his father's apologies and confessions, and shook his head.

"Why now, Dad? Why so long?"

"This is when you came back. You haven't given us a chance to say so before. I didn't believe it when they told me, and then there you were, at the party." His father stepped in, looked closer, his eyes narrowing.

"You seem different, Daniel. Harder. Not that there's anything bad about that in a man, but you can be too hard, so that nothing gets past the surface. I don't want that to happen. Don't want to have been the cause of it."

"You're not, Dad. It's…the job. We have to do things you probably can't imagine, and don't want to. I don't belong here anymore. I appreciate what you said, but it's not your fault—I could have stopped Stew. I could have gone to his training officer, told him about Stewart and water, done something more than I did."

The blazing fire of indignation had his father's face red as a brick. "You will not blame yourself for this. It's an injustice to your brother, it makes him less of a man to say he couldn't make his own decisions, even if those decisions killed him."

Daniel was taken aback, and let his father's words soak in, though Arthur MacAlister was far from finished.

"And of course you belong here, always did. I botched by putting too much on you about Stewart, but you botched by never coming home—even if you hated me, you could have seen the rest of the family. And if you leave them again now, that's on you, too. But I hope you won't."

"I don't hate you, Dad, but it's much more complicated than you know."

"You listen to me, Daniel. Why is it that every new generation thinks they've invented the damned wheel? Do you think you're the first in our history to make sacrifices for your country? Do you think anything you've done is so shocking your family wouldn't have you? Maybe you think that, but you'd be wrong. Because we know something you apparently don't."

"And what's that?"

"That you're a good man, a strong man, made of the same blood and bone as that baby there. No matter what it is you've done, I have no doubt that you did it for the best of reasons."

"You really believe that?"

"I do. You're one of us. I believed it about Stewart, and I believe it about Alan—I guess I have some apologizing to do to him, as well. Steven is a solid man—I guess the idea just takes some getting used to."

Daniel slanted a smile at his father, amazed. Their Scot ancestry was littered with rebels and warriors, men of violence and honor, who defended country, home and hearth. Daniel couldn't help but feel a spark of pride that his father might think of him in those terms, and the weight of guilt that he'd carried for a decade started to lessen.

"We should go rejoin the women. Check on Anna."

And with that, Daniel walked out with his father's hand on his shoulder and felt part of his family again, if only for a moment.

12

THE GULF BETWEEN THEM was evident in Daniel's silence, the distance that signaled he was there in body, but not in spirit, Risa thought sadly as she and Daniel headed back to his car. What had happened with Arthur? Daniel hadn't said a word, but they'd seemed more relaxed around each other when they'd emerged from the neonatal unit. Risa didn't think it was her place to ask. Personal questions were things lovers shared, and she couldn't claim that status anymore.

"So what now?" She broke the silence as they reached the car, looking at him over the slope of the roof.

He stared at her, pausing, and then shook his head. "We have a way out—meeting a plane in four hours."

"Where are we going?"

"I don't know yet—just somewhere away from here. In hiding—we need to stay out of sight until I can get more information about what's happening."

Slipping into the passenger seat, she turned to him, unsure what to say but needing to say something, when his cell rang. As he listened, reassured by whoever was on the other end that their connection was secure, she could almost see his features change. Though she could only hear one side of the conversation, she knew the look—he was hearing news he didn't particularly like. His sensual lips set in a flat line as he hung up.

"Well, we have one lead," he said as soon as he clicked the phone shut. "The phone call to Ben Richter came from a guy named Gunter Reimann, a longtime officer in the BND—German Intelligence. Ben is one of them."

"Ben's a spy?" Risa breathed the words out, putting two and two together and not liking four. "Do you think he was watching me?"

Daniel nodded. "Most likely. However, he never made direct contact with you—not until after you approached him. He went months without saying a word to you, right?"

She nodded. She hadn't been the most social creature during that time, but it would have been easy enough for Ben to make contact somewhere around the building if he had really been determined.

"I don't think he was after you, specifically—he doesn't know about you. He might have been assigned to watch you because of your association with someone else they were after."

"But who? I don't know anyone."

"You know Dr. Laslow. Maybe better than anyone."

Risa sat back in her seat, processing the theory Daniel was positing. So, she'd been watching Ben, but Ben had also been watching her. But what would Ben's interest in Dr. Laslow be?

"Do we know what side Ben is on?"

He shrugged wearily. "Not for sure."

Daniel was pensive, and clearly doubtful. "We'll have to have someone dig deeper, find out what the connections could be, but in the meantime, we have to stay out of sight."

"I have a gut feeling where we should go."

"How's that?"

"I don't know. The flashback I had to the lab explosion, when you pulled me out. I was inside the network, and I hit something, like a trip wire, that set off the electromagnetic blast. Like it had been set there. I saw something, and it triggered the blast."

"What did you see?"

"That's it—I can't remember. It's like a blank spot when I try to figure out what it was, but that doesn't make any sense. I can remember everything else so clearly, even you, though I was almost unconscious."

"So you think that blank spot could have something to do with what's happening now? With Laslow?"

She shrugged. "I don't know. I guess I just feel like there's unfinished business, like the only way I might be able to remember is going back to that spot."

"Makes sense. That's where we'll go, then."

Risa was shocked for a second. "You believe me? Just like that?"

"For all the training I've had, I always trust my gut. If yours is telling you this is where we have to go, I'm willing to trust that, and even if we're wrong, it gets us far away from here, and we'll buy some time to figure out our next step."

He started the car and pulled out of the garage

without another word, and Risa sat back, silent, as well. She didn't know what was coming next, but she wasn't giving up easily on the new life she'd found, whether Daniel remained in it or not.

DANIEL PROMPTED Risa with a beckoning gesture as they stood among the deserted sand dunes, a low sliver of a moon visible in the dark sky above them. It was the middle of the night, and they still had three hours before they had to meet their plane. Daniel believed the time was best spent giving Risa a little impromptu training, since they didn't know what was coming next.

She may have gone on missions before, but she'd never had to do hand-to-hand. In spite of her super-strength, the powers-that-be had never wanted to risk her real value to them, which was her mind- and machine-reading abilities. But if they were going into this situation, not knowing what was waiting for them, she needed to know at least the basics now. He hoped it would be enough.

She was standing about five feet away, directly in front of him, lit only by the headlights of the car. He didn't dare take them anywhere more public. He gestured her closer one more time.

"C'mon, Risa, you have to get in here, close. Fighting isn't about standing five feet away from your opponent. You have to be aggressive, strike first, strike hard, keep on striking. You've got to be in close."

"I've taken some martial arts, Daniel. I know how to defend myself."

Why was she being so difficult? Was she so determined to keep her physical distance from him that she'd risk her life before touching him? The idea pissed him off and he stopped waiting for her, moving in fast, closing his hands around her throat and pulling her roughly against him in a split second, her eyes wide as she struggled to get away.

"Hunch!" he ordered, but she twisted and kicked to no avail—her moves were instinctive and ineffective. She may have been taught some martial arts, but she'd obviously never had to worry about defending herself physically, and her body had no muscle memory of how to do so.

"Hunch your shoulders!" he ordered again, more harshly, not taking his hands from her throat even though she made a tiny gasping noise. This time she did as he said and hunched up sharply, loosening his grip somewhat and making it harder for him to apply pressure.

"Good. Now follow through like this." He brought her hand up, and showed her how to further use her body to unbalance her assailant and redirect the attack. They repeated the moves until he was satisfied.

He released her, hoping he'd made his point.

"Now, grab my arms."

She hesitated, and then reached forward, closing her hands around his wrists tightly. Within seconds he'd loosened her grip and stepped in such a way that he had her arms trapped and was in perfect striking distance, delivering a combination of feints to her face so quickly she only stared and blinked. He stopped, but kept her trapped up close to him, not relinquishing his hold. It just felt too damned good to be touching her again. If this was all they could share, he'd take it.

"Did you see what I did there?"

She nodded, and for good measure, he tugged her in just a little closer, even though it wasn't completely necessary. "Even though you attacked me, I took control of you—opened you up, disabled your hold, struck hard and fast. You want to neutralize them first, then attack. Or if you have time, if you see them coming at you, you attack first. Don't think, just attack. They'll expect defense, not a counterattack, especially from someone your size. Get in close, go for any vulnerable point, don't hold back. Let's try both."

"Okay, let me try."

He stepped back, searching around the beach as if making sure no one was watching, and then suddenly grabbed her again, feeling her move against him, mimicking the moves he'd used on her. But she was holding him at a distance, not committing to the action, and he defeated her easily, once again pulling her up close, forcing the contact she seemed to be intent on avoiding. Holding her immobile, his mouth was by the sweet skin of her ear, and he leaned the fraction of an inch it took to touch the tender flesh with his lips, speaking in low tones,

"Fighting is a lot like sex, Risa—you have to get in close, you have to lose your inhibitions and go for it, willing to touch your opponent anywhere, eager to counter any move they make. You can't be afraid of the contact. If you are, then you won't be any good. With sex, failure to commit means you may not get as much pleasure from the experience as you could. In fighting, it can mean your life."

She pulled against him again, and the way she strained and moved to escape his hold might have been ineffective from a training standpoint, but it was wreaking havoc on his libido—his body was at painful attention, and he shifted his hips slightly so that his erection came in full contact with her hip, then he leaned closer.

Unsure what he was trying to do—turn her on, piss her off or just assuage the desire that was burning a path through his bloodstream—he moved his mouth over the skin of her cheek, ignoring the sound of protest she made as he closed his lips over hers, forcing a kiss that had her body straining toward him though she tried to move her lips away from his. Finally, he stepped back.

"You bastard, don't you dare force me—"

"They'll do worse if they get hold of you," he stated flatly, ignoring the way her shirt had pulled from her shoulder, and how the desire was sparking in her eyes along with the anger. Not allowing her to get her bearings, he came in again, grabbed her and hauled her up. This time she positioned her body in just the right way and spun away from him. Before coming up from underneath just as he'd shown her, for a second he thought she might not pull the hard strike, then her elbow rose to his jaw.

The victory and satisfaction flaring in her eyes only fueled his own response. He was proud of her, she'd done it, but his orders for close contact were doubling back on him—his body refused to stop acknowledging hers, and the rush of their violent contact seemed to turn him on even more. Her life was on the line—both of their lives, and that of a government scientist. He shouldn't be thinking about sex, of all things.

"That was good. Try it again at a different angle."

He came in again and again, and each time, though she was a little clunky here and there, she got faster, more effective, more deadly. She was small, but even without her superpowers she was strong. Breathing heavily from the exercise, he nodded in satisfaction with her progress.

"Now, here… You want to be able to respond from any position. Don't let your opponent get the upper hand. What we're going to do is much like wrestling, escaping a hold, getting out from underneath an opponent—ready?"

She was more ready this time—maybe more ready than he was when he swept her legs out and landed on top of her in the sand and grass, his long body pinning down her smaller, lithe one. Wanting her seemed to be as much of a reflex as fighting was—he hardened, pressed in between her taut thighs and thought from the stifled moan she made that she was either as turned on as he was, or hurt from the fall.

"Are you all right? Did we land too hard?"

Her voice was breathless as she responded, "No, I'm fine. You just…knocked the wind out of me." Then she turned all business. "How do I get you off of me?"

He showed her several moves that would help her escape from a similar pin, and they practiced until she started moving reflexively, finding her own ways of applying the motions that worked best for her. Pride was apparent in her voice when she not only managed to escape his final hold, but pin him soundly in return. He smiled at her straddling him victoriously, his beautiful woman warrior.

The company had made a huge mistake in not keeping her on; she was a quick study. If they lived through this, maybe she could come back and be a field agent, but did she even want that anymore?

The question that was more pressing in his mind, however, as she didn't move from her position over him, was, did she still want *him?* No doubt they had their issues, but he couldn't deny his response to her, physically and otherwise. It was clear that he was falling for Risa Remington. Hard. Her words kept coming back to him, torturing him, tempting him. *I'm falling in love with you....*

She stared down at him, picking up on some silent vibe, neither of them saying a word. He didn't know what to expect, but it wasn't having her lean down and gently touch her mouth to his. The soft kiss electrified him, making him want more, but he stemmed the impulse, closing his hands over her forearms and pushing her back slightly.

"Don't mess with me, Risa."

"I'm not. I—I missed touching you. Even if it was just for a day, and I'm probably a fool to admit it, to give you that kind of power over me, but it's true."

She slid down, planted her head against his chest, and he slid his arms around her, marveling at the change, expecting her to break away any second, but she just spoke softly, "I thought you didn't want to touch me anymore."

She took a breath, continuing, as if she had to say what she said quickly, or not at all. "I thought, after what happened, and then what happened in the room, that there was no way I could feel this for you again, but for some reason, I can't seem to stop—"

"I know. Me, too," he interrupted, running a hand down over her hair, soothing her after the exertion of their fighting, both physical and otherwise. "I'm so sorry for what I did, Risa—I don't know what to do about it, but I can't seem to stop wanting you. But it's more than that. I don't want to say what, but…more."

"Have you ever been in love, Daniel?"

The whispered question caught him off guard again, and he wasn't completely sure how to answer—was he in love? Were they? He'd always imagined love to be a gentler, tamer thing—but those words hardly applied to the passion and degree of wanting he felt toward Risa. Did they apply to his urge to protect her? To make sure she was safe? Was that love?

He took her hands, hoping the chance to have the kind of closeness they'd had before hadn't disappeared. Shutting his eyes, he tried to open his mind to her. Without words, she seemed to understand, and a tear fell from her eye, splashing on his cheek.

He felt her soften against him, and he moved up against her, showing her the extent of his desire.

Whatever was between them, the intense need wouldn't be slaked by sex alone. At the moment, he didn't care what it took. He would do anything, give her anything— take everything.

They were alone. They didn't know what was going to happen next, and he wanted her. He wanted one last perfect moment with no barriers between them, regardless of what came next. If he was in love with her, so be it. If love was what made her feel so incredibly good as she moved over him and against him, their bodies seeking the kind of mating their mouths were engaged in, then he was all for it. She clutched his hair in her fingers, breathed him in, moaning against him, but frustration edged her voice.

"I can't see anything, Daniel. I don't know what happened that time, before, but my powers are gone. Really, they are." She sounded disappointed, but also relieved, and he took her hands in his, lifting them to his mouth.

"You don't have to see inside my mind, Risa, though I don't mind if you do. Let me show you how I feel," he barely managed to murmur, and with his skills far advancing hers, he shifted and moved her from her dominant position, pushing off to a standing position and swinging her up into his arms. Daniel felt like an old-time movie hero carrying her back to the car. He captured her mouth again, unable to stop touching or kissing her for a second.

They didn't make it inside the cramped quarters of the vehicle, but instead, he set her on the hood, warm from the engine running, the shine of the headlights broken by their tangled legs. He laid her back, spreading her legs with his and settling in between even though she was still completely dressed. Leaning over, he cradled her head in his hands, kissing her so deeply, so completely, that he felt taken somewhere else, lifted out of the moment.

Her arms were wound tightly around his neck and she brought her legs up, cinching them around his waist and moving against him in a motion that soon had him agreeing that the kissing, while extraordinary, was not enough—not nearly. However, he didn't want to stop.

He removed his hands gently, lowering her head to the hood, and used his free hands to dispose of her garments as efficiently as he could without breaking the contact of their mouths. His own needs roared to life as his hands moved over her naked skin, and he could feel the goose bumps where the breeze tickled her hot skin and puckered her sweet little nipples, begging him to pay attention.

He moved away from the kiss, lowering his mouth to the dark pink buds that tempted him, sucking lightly, drawing the increasingly hard nubs between his teeth as she writhed beneath him, demanding more. And he planned to give her just what she asked for—he wanted to give her everything.

For all the times they'd been together over the past week, he found himself wanting to kiss away every possible hurt, every doubt he'd had, every harsh comment. He wanted them to burn clean in the fire of the passion that was quickly consuming him, and start anew.

Lowering down, he lifted her legs up over his shoulders, tracing an indolent path down the inside of her legs with his tongue before settling in between. Parting the fleshy folds of her sex, he planted kisses as hot and deep there as he had on her lips, and opened her wider, his palms on her cheeks, leaving no part of her untouched, unkissed.

He knew just how to make her come, and felt the shudder rack her body as she cried out, arching upwards, fitting to him even more tightly as her legs gripped him, and he sent her over again. The well of giving was deep, and he didn't stop until she dug her hands into his hair, begging him, demanding and pleading that he join her.

He reached down, quickly releasing himself, his cock jutting forward eagerly, finding her unerringly and pushing inside. When his shaft was buried tightly within her, he drew Risa into his arms, catching her slack, satisfied body against his, holding her close as he started to move. Their joining was reconciliation and forgiveness—promise and passion all at once—and he felt all of the emotions that had been muddying his life coalesce and clarify.

"Oh, honey…Risa. That's it, just like that. Can you feel how perfect we are together?" he encouraged as she moved with him in synchronous rhythm.

She pulled him to her and found his mouth, kissing her own moisture from his skin before delving her tongue into his mouth with such sultry abandon his knees nearly buckled and he almost came on the spot. But he wanted it to last, being connected to her in every way. He knew she might be able to read him again, and he didn't care—he was utterly open to her. But he was also more than willing to show her and tell her how he felt—she didn't need to read his mind for that.

Slowing down, he braced his legs and thrust at a rate that had her digging her fingers into his back, panting against his neck with short, feminine gasps as she started to clench him tighter, teetering on the edge of her climax. He curled one hand under the curve of her backside angling her in just such a way that he could thrust even deeper, making sure his length came into contact with every part of her.

She moaned through her release within seconds, the strong contractions milking his own response, and he buried his face in the fragrant hollow of her neck, a stinging sensation at the back of his eyes accompanying the most emphatic orgasm he'd ever experienced.

"I love you, baby…I love you more than life."

She still clung to him, arms and legs wound around him so tightly. He didn't want to leave her, either, to face the daunting reality waiting for them on the other side.

She drew back first, looking up at him and leaning in to lay her cheek against his in a tender gesture that melted him.

"I love you, too, Daniel."

"Risa, you've brought me back to life. I've never felt so connected to anyone."

She murmured something unintelligible back to him, gathering him close, and he knew she felt the connection between them, too. His soul seemed to be expanding, standing there half-naked in the dunes, holding her close, saying nothing. Words were extraneous at this point.

As dawn started edging its way over the sky behind them, they drew apart, and silently put their clothes on. Daniel faced her, the love he'd only just discovered filling him with fear for what was about to happen—he knew he couldn't have discovered these new feelings at a worse time, but it wasn't something he would have traded for the world.

"It's time to go." She moved past him briskly, stopping to squeeze his hand tightly once, and smiled up at him. He felt new determination. He would do whatever he had to do to make sure he would see that smile every day long past this one. There was no way they would fail.

13

RISA LOOKED OUT of the window of the small private jet—apparently, Daniel still had powerful friends that were outside the realm of Jack White's knowledge. They were only minutes from landing in Nevada, near the desert where they would drive out to the lab where she had lost her powers, and almost her life. She was unafraid, but anxious to get to the spot—somehow she felt they'd find their answers there.

Daniel was sound asleep in the seat beside her. She watched him, enjoying how different his face was while he was sleeping, more relaxed and boyish. He'd told her he loved her. She'd never felt as connected to anyone, even when she'd been reading their minds, and it was a little frightening. The connection that happened when your heart was involved, not just your mind, was deeper than she ever expected.

It had been replaying in her mind since he'd said it, robbing her of any sleep as she pondered what it meant. Did everything stay the same? Would he still leave? Had something changed? What exactly did saying you loved someone mean?

She'd approached the emotion welling inside of her

from every angle, and couldn't say it was all she'd imagined it was cracked up to be. Didn't being in love with someone make you happy? Current circumstances aside, shouldn't she be happy to be in love with Daniel, and happy that he loved her? Wasn't that how it was supposed to be? When people in the movies and in books fell in love, they felt great, invincible, and they knew everything would turn out right. She didn't feel that way.

Instead, she felt anxious and fearful. They were operating in the dark; it wasn't like previous missions where they had complete briefings and backup—this time they were on their own, and even their own people were out for them.

"Those look like some heavy thoughts you're carrying around," Daniel whispered from his seat, waking up and stretching as they were informed over an intercom to fasten their belts for landing.

"Just thinking about what's going to happen next."

He took her to mean their mission, not their relationship, and she didn't bother to correct him.

"We'll get settled and wait, see if we detect any activity, and then approach."

"I thought maybe we should contact the BMD—the Germans. See if we could get their help?"

He pursed his lips, considering her idea, but shaking his head. "We don't know who we can trust right now, or what their interest is—maybe when we know more."

She nodded. The plane landed smoothly. They'd left in darkness, and arrived near the Nevada Black Rock

Desert just past dawn. Risa mused that it felt as if it had been dark for an awful long time.

A Jeep was waiting for them, and they hopped in, Daniel taking the wheel while Risa consulted the maps provided for them. They stopped at a gas station and donned the desert travel gear that had been provided in the backseat. There were tents, water, sleeping bags, first-aid kits—pretty much everything that they would need for a desert camping expedition, including two-way radios, since there was no cell phone coverage here. Daniel's contacts left him well prepared. Then they were off, bumping across the flat sand.

Risa gazed around her at the desert plants and rocks starting to take shape in the brighter morning light. The area was perennial dry lake bed, one of the largest areas of flat land on earth.

It wasn't long before the crumpled metal shell of the hangar came into view—it was completely dilapidated, barely recognizable. Decades earlier, the old hangar had once been a landing strip and business center for South American drug planes. Daniel parked the Jeep behind a low dune, quickly pulled a tent from the back and popped it into place. They needed to establish some cover, just in case anyone was watching.

She followed suit, grabbing the coolers and a tripod for good measure. They'd look to be vacationers out taking photos of the desert landscape. Hats, sunglasses and new clothes would mask their appearance from all but the closest inspection.

"We'll hang out here, see if there's any activity and

move in for a closer view...." He opened a cold soda and handed it to her, and she sat on the tailgate, trying to appear casual as she glanced around.

Risa tilted her head back, enjoying the warmth of the desert sun that rose in the clear sky—she always did like the heat. Daniel rummaged in the back of the truck, preparing supplies and weapons, handing her a sleek automatic pistol under cover of a shirt draped on his arm. "You know how to use this?"

She took it, weighing it in her hand. "I was given some instruction, though I never carried a gun on missions."

"I guess you wouldn't have needed it."

"I was never on the front line—that was your job. You were the muscle, I was the talent," she joked, grinning cheekily.

"Well, hold on to it for now. Hopefully, you won't have any reason to use it."

She nodded, watching him snap a camera onto the tripod, adjusting the zoom and looking at the hangar and its surrounding area.

"It's hard to tell. Could be tire tracks around the hangar—the sand has covered them. But if they're there, they're relatively fresh."

"Could be vacationers."

"Yeah. Or not. We'll come in from the west, there's more cover from that direction. Take some water and a camera—we're just tourists out for a jaunt."

She nodded and followed him away from the truck, walking out into the rocky landscape. The only other time she'd been here was in the dead of night—the night of her accident. She didn't know what she'd expected to feel as they approached the hangar, but she didn't feel much. It was strange, considering this was the place where her life had changed forever. Daniel touched her shoulder.

"So far, so good. No one seems to be aware of our presence."

He turned and jogged to the hangar, gesturing for her to follow. Lifting the camera, she took some random shots of Daniel and the area around him, as she assumed any tourist might do. At one point, he bent down, inspecting the ground, and then beckoned her closer. She joined him, bending in close to see what he'd found.

"Fresh footsteps—several of them," he whispered. "We're not the only ones interested in this site—looks like your gut feelings could be right on."

She felt a flush of pleasure at the confidence and approval in his voice. They followed the footsteps while appearing to simply inspect the broken-down building.

"They stop here, but they don't backtrack."

In spite of several warning signs to stay away and keep out, Daniel pulled at a section of loose metal, and it gave way easily—leaning in, they could both see clear, undisturbed sets of footprints in the dirt and dust inside. With one last look around, they stepped inside and Daniel replaced the metal section.

"Empty," Risa declared, walking to the spot where she remembered the floor panel lifting to expose the hidden floor duct where they'd scooted down pipes into the underground lab the first time. It was still there. She looked at Daniel and he shrugged.

"Might as well. We've come this far. Me first."

She stepped back as he sat on the edge of the hole and lowered himself down, clipping a bright miner's light to his belt for visibility. She watched the point of light descend and then lowered herself after him, holding her breath. It was unlikely that anyone was here if they hadn't been detained already.

As she climbed down the PVC pipes that ran along the small space, her mind flooded with images from her flashback. She stopped, taking a breath, feeling dizzy. She could not afford another blackout, not here, not now.

She heard Daniel's boots hit the floor below her, and seconds later she joined him. It was pitch-black except for their lights, and they stood in place, perusing the wreckage around them. The lab had been dismantled and destroyed. The EMP hadn't any effect on the building, but the CIA had come in afterward and gutted the place. It was just a shell of the high-tech work space it had once been.

"There's nothing here," she breathed out, discouraged. Had this all just been a waste of time?

"Are you remembering anything more?"

She shook her head, her confidence in her "gut feelings" fading. This could all be a desperate goose chase.

"Let's look around anyway. There could be some clues."

She'd just started moving forward when a noise caught her attention.

"Did you hear that?"

Daniel looked at her, stock-still, and they waited—
it came again. A shuffling—maybe an animal? Or
maybe something else.

The door to the chamber where the blast had been
set off was partly open, and the sound seemed to be
coming from there. They went forward cautiously. The
chamber was a large cylindrical room. An inner room
encased in unbreakable glass was inside a larger one
where the controls resided. The glass was unbroken,
though everything else was gone. Consoles were
covered with dust, and there were gaping holes where
the equipment used to be.

Risa felt a chill go down her spine—the last time she
was here, she'd started to explore the networks, to gather
what information she could about the experiments and
tests that were being performed. The next thing she
knew, she was waking up in a hospital bed.

"Are you okay?" Daniel appeared at her side.

"It just hit me, how could they know?"

"Know what?"

"When I was inside the networks, it was like there was
a trap, waiting for me—like someone knew I was coming.
I felt like I saw something, and then the blast set off."

"Could it have been a normal virus, some glitch that
set off the blast?"

"No. It was deliberate—hard to explain, but trust me."

"That definitely puts a new spin on things."

They heard the sound again, accompanied by a distinctly human moan, and bolted to the inner chamber
where just inside the door they found someone bound,

gagged and shoved into a dirty corner, his head covered with a burlap sack. Risa fell to her knees before the figure and felt the breath whoosh from her when she pulled the bag away, expecting to see Dr. Laslow, and instead finding a dirty, beaten, barely conscious Ben Richter.

"Ben!" Daniel and Risa exclaimed simultaneously, pausing only a split second before removing his gag and bonds, and offering him water from the bottles clipped to their belts, but he could barely acknowledge their presence or speak.

"He needs a doctor, fast," Daniel muttered, doing a quick inspection of his pulse and pupils.

"I guess we got the right place, but the wrong person," Risa whispered, trying to help Daniel move Ben's limp form to a semicomfortable position. "What happened? He's banged up, but he doesn't look that badly beaten."

Daniel did a quick inspection of Ben's arms, ripping up his sleeves, his expression grim. Ben's inner forearm was swollen and red. "He's been injected with something. Looks pretty toxic. Amazing he's still alive, but we have to get help."

Risa gasped, nearly toppling back in surprise when Ben lurched forward, grabbing her forearm, his eyes open and wild.

"*You!* He wants to be you—he always wanted to be you. Has collected everything, has studied you—he killed them. He did it…wanted you to himself."

Daniel gently broke Ben's grasp and eased him back, though the incoherent man struggled slightly before he passed out again, mumbling in German. Risa rubbed her arm, shocked, startled by the incident and more shaken than she wanted to admit.

"What was that about?" Daniel eyed her closely. "Are you all right?"

"He's obviously under the influence of some kind of psychotropic drug. He doesn't know what he's saying," Risa stated, standing and shaking off her nerves. "One of us has to go for help."

Daniel nodded. She knew it would blow their mission, and their cover, but Ben needed help, and that had to come first. Daniel stood.

"I'll go call in from the radio. Hopefully they can get here in time, and we can move out before they do."

"I'll stay with Ben."

Daniel paused. "You're sure? He's unstable. And he seems fixated on you for some reason."

"He's weak, drugged. How much harm could he do?"

Daniel looked reluctant, but they had to make a decision. "Fine. I'll be back within ten minutes—if I'm not, something's gone bad. Get out. Don't wait for me."

She nodded, her heart in her throat. She wanted to grab him to keep him next to her, to throw her arms around him and say…what? Swallowing those impulses, she knelt by Ben, and looked up at Daniel.

"You'll be back. I'll wait here."

"Ten minutes," was all he said, and he was gone.

Risa watched Ben, wondering what had happened to him, and who had done this. In spite of what she'd said to Daniel, she'd felt Ben's intent to talk to her, his recognition of her. He knew something. He'd said someone had "killed them." Killed who?

Outside the chamber, Daniel's footsteps signaled his return. That was fast—he'd only been gone a few minutes. She breathed a sigh of relief as he turned the corner of the doorway into the inner chamber. Her heart lurched when she saw two men following behind him, with guns. No…three men with him.

Dr. Laslow came in behind the two with guns, looking odd in his crisp white lab coat among the dust and grime of the site. He looked at Risa on the floor with Ben, and just smiled.

"Risa. I'm so happy to see you. An unexpected pleasure." He gestured to the other men, and ordered, "Bring them."

He turned his back and disappeared out of the room, the two men pointing with their guns for Risa to join Daniel. She shook her head.

"Ben needs help—we can't leave him."

One man trained his gun on Daniel's head, and she got the message. She stood and looked down at Ben one more time. He had passed out, probably comatose, maybe dead. She had to put her energies into saving her own skin, and Daniel's.

"Okay, okay," she reassured them, standing slowly. "I'm coming."

One man crossed to her, patted her down rather rudely—maybe enjoying the process a little too much—and found her gun. Crap.

They filed through the narrow doorway, and into

another entryway masked by the wreckage—beyond which housed an entirely new lab. She walked into the shining new facility with no small bit of surprise. Laslow was standing among gleaming new equipment, smiling as if he were showing off his new home to friends.

"How do you like it?"

Risa bit her lip as a sharp pain shot through her forehead. Oh, no—she didn't need a collapse right now. She had to try to stay functional for both of their sakes. But the pounding became insistent, and her step faltered.

"Feeling a little off, Risa, dear? Well, we'll fix that up in no time," Laslow crooned, and she felt a shiver wrap around her spine.

"You weren't kidnapped," she managed.

"Hardly. Though it was easy enough to make it appear that way. I thought it would implicate you— they were on pins and needles about you already—and take care of you for good." He directed a cool gaze to Daniel. "That was supposed to be your job, I hear."

Daniel stood still, absolutely still, and said nothing. Risa tried to make eye contact, but Daniel didn't take his eyes off of Dr. Laslow, who shrugged, looking around the room.

"Anyway, you see what the right funding will accomplish. Now I have everything I need to finish my project."

"What project?"

Laslow looked surprised. "Why, you, of course. You've always been the center and purpose of my existence."

Risa closed her eyes, fighting back the pain—why did this have to happen now?

"You used me. You didn't care about me."

"On the contrary—I cared more than you can know. You were the only one I could study from birth. I'd met your mother too late to observe her development, study the changes in her brain composition and her chemical balances. But you—you I had from the beginning. And I'll be there at your end, too. Fitting, wouldn't you say?"

"I don't understand what you want—or why you are doing any of this."

"Is it really that hard to understand? I've spent my entire life in the shadows, in the background, watching from a distance as you got the gratitude and the celebration for only doing what comes naturally to you— did anyone ever realize my part? How you were able to do what you did because of my help? My mentorship? Hardly."

"You were my doctor. You were supposed to take care of me."

"And I did that, didn't I? Very well. But I'm taking care of myself, too." He picked up a syringe, holding it up between his eyes as he looked at her. She felt nauseated. "Soon, the world will see you aren't all that special—or rather, you weren't. You're just normal now, aren't you? Boring and normal like the rest of us."

"What is that? What have you done?"

"I've studied, waited, and now I will triumph. I've performed a thousand experiments, but I'm getting closer every day. This, my dear, is a compound that, when injected into a recipient under the right conditions, which require a rather sizable electric current being shot through the body, will transfer your abilities to any subject."

Risa felt everything spin a little, her mind growing hazy, but she fought it. "You can replicate my powers?"

"I can't—not yet—but I'm getting closer. Having you come here works out beautifully. I can take more DNA samples, and thanks to you and Agent MacAlister, I'll have two more very apt subjects for my experiment."

"You want to give me my powers back? Why?"

"Oh, no, I don't. In fact, once I can tell if the serum has worked or not, I'll be sure to overdose you, and you won't last long after that—the human system simply can't handle the toxins. Illustrated by your friend's reaction—he won't last much longer, even with his stout German disposition."

"You son of a bitch. You did this to me—you set off the blast…I saw…I saw *you*." Her mind was blipping in and out of images, sliding back and forth between the present and the past, and she wobbled, feeling arms grip her, holding her steady. She looked up into Daniel's eyes.

"Yes, it was necessary. I needed you out of the way, and I needed to see how and if your abilities could be neutralized. We all have our limits, our kryptonite, if you will—I had to find yours."

"I'm remembering…"

"Oh, that's not good." He tsked as he shook his head at her. "I guess you can remember that you saw the evidence of my work in the networks you were so industrially exploring. But I was always one step ahead— I'd planned for that, just in case. I didn't expect you to survive, but I was able to handle that, as well. Old-fashioned brainwashing techniques worked to bury anything you might remember."

"It's why she's been suffering these headaches, the flashbacks…her mind has been struggling to show her the truth," Daniel declared.

Laslow shrugged, nodding in agreement. "Most likely. The mind is an amazing instrument. But if that's the case, you can see why I can't have either one of you around. What I'm doing is too important. Too profitable."

"You plan to sell this serum when you perfect it?"

"As well as dosing myself, yes. Once I have it, I'll be unstoppable. But enough of this chitchat…."

Daniel felt Risa sag farther in his grasp. She was losing the fight, and he searched desperately for a way to swing this to his advantage. Hoisting her, he did the only thing he could and pushed her forward, hard, into Laslow's arms, knocking the syringe to the floor, and toppling the doctor with her. At the same time, he kicked back, catching one of the guards in the knee, and then threw himself bodily into the other.

The guy he landed on was down—Daniel had hit him hard. The goon was out for the count, but the other one was scuffling to his feet, scrambling for his gun. Daniel reached it first. He directed it at the man's head, sending him a warning glance, and turned to see where Laslow had gone.

Risa wasn't unconscious, but she was in imminent danger—Laslow had pinned her, and was holding the syringe threateningly above her, catching Daniel's eye with a knowing look. Daniel weighed his options within split seconds. At this point, it was more important to take Laslow alive, to capture him and reveal his hidden operation—not to mention the people he was working for—than to save Risa. That's what the agent in him said. Daniel's life and the decisions he'd made often balanced on measuring the good of the many against the good of the one or the few.

But even so, there was no way he was letting anything happen to Risa—regardless of the consequences. That was what the man who loved her decided.

"I suggest you lower that gun, Agent, or she'll die a very horrible death," Laslow said, his voice shaking with cold determination as he brought the syringe closer to Risa's throat.

Daniel started to lower the gun, and the guard moved closer to disarm him, when a loud shriek filled the room, and Daniel watched Laslow jerk as Risa used the moves he'd taught her and pushed him back, snatching the syringe from his hand, and battling him for control. Daniel tried to find a clean shot, to help her, but the guard was on him, and he fired into the ceiling, setting off an alarm, but not helping Risa.

However, when he was clear to look up again, he saw she didn't need his help—she sagged back against a cabinet, tears streaming down her face, her body shaking, with Laslow shuddering at her feet, the syringe he'd held stabbed into his heart. He buckled in seizures, his eyes wide before they closed, and he stilled.

So much for taking him alive. But Risa was okay, and

that's all that mattered. Daniel crossed the room, dropped the gun and pulled her close.

"Oh, baby, it's okay. We did it."

"I've killed him—they won't believe me, Daniel, they won't believe I wasn't involved...."

He tilted her face up to meet his. "They will. We'll make them. This place is evidence enough, and there's Ben—if he's still alive. We need to get help. Can I leave you for a moment?"

Risa nodded, wiping the tears from her face, and though Daniel hesitated to leave her again, he knew he had to help the man in the other room, if help was still needed.

As he stood to leave, she reached up and took his hand, and he stopped, looking down into her tearstained face.

"I love you, Daniel. No matter what happens after this, I love you with all my heart."

He bent, brushing his lips over her knuckles, the love clear in his eyes for her to see. He dropped her hand, leaving to see if there was anything to be done for Ben Richter. Then he'd see about making sure that none of this ever touched Risa's life again.

14

Three months later...

"HAPPY BIRTHDAY to you, happy birthday to you..." The song filled the backyard, the late summer heat easing off for the evening, fireflies speckling the air around them as Risa contemplated the cake set before her. She turned twenty-seven today, and it felt as if she stood at the brink of an entirely new life. The cake was huge, and looked delicious—chocolate. Her favorite.

"Blow out the candles, sweetheart, before the yard catches on fire," Daniel teased, leaning in to kiss her hair. His family, Ben and Kristy gathered around and encouraged her to do the same. She hadn't had a birthday cake since her parents had died, let alone a party. She felt tears sting behind her eyes; that happened a lot these days, for happy reasons, mostly, and she didn't mind if anyone saw.

She blew out the candles, smiling when everyone clapped, and took the large cake knife Dorothy handed her.

"You cut the cake, dear. I'll do ice cream."

It was all so *normal* she thought as she slid the knife through the layers—so wonderfully, gloriously, amazingly normal. Though the past months had held some challenges, as she worked with the agency to sort out what had happened and tried to process what had been done to her and her family by Dr. Laslow. It was a nightmare, and if it weren't for Daniel's support, his family and her friends, she wouldn't have gotten through it.

"Cut me a big piece," Ben requested, eyeing the cake with no small amount of food lust. He loved chocolate. She gladly did as he requested. He'd been retired from the BND for nerve damage caused by the injections and electric shock Laslow had inflicted on him. Daniel had reached help in time, and with the remaining serum they'd found in the lab, the government doctors had been able to save Ben, but some of the damage was permanent. He could no longer work in the field, and had moved to America to be with Kristy. The four of them had become close friends through the ordeal.

Ben spoke again, enthusiastic even with a mouthful of chocolate cake. "Oh! Kristy has your gift from us—here they come!"

Kristy walked quickly across the yard, giggling as she tried to hold on to the wiggling puppy in her arms, avoiding its playful licks. When she got closer, she put the little black furball down, and it joyfully took advantage of its freedom, galloping around the yard, eventually sitting down right at Risa's feet, as if he had found his rightful place.

"He's mine?" She reached down to pet the sleek black fur, and the puppy stretched, enjoying every second, gazing up at her in blatant adoration.

"He's yours—Daniel said you liked dogs."

Risa picked the puppy up, squeezing him to her in spite of his wriggles.

"He's gorgeous—thank you so much. He's perfect!"

The pup wiggled free, heading for the baby, William, home for over a month now, safely cradled in his play yard with Anna and Brandon doting nearby. As baby and puppy watched each other, the puppy frolicked and tossed itself head over heels in his excitement around the outside of the play yard.

"I'll name him Rolly."

"It fits him. May you both have long years, and good health." Kristy leaned in to kiss Risa on the cheek, then returned to Ben's side and swiped some of his cake.

When Arthur popped open the large bottle of champagne on the table, everyone cheered and stepped forward for a glass. Risa sat back, watching them all happily, especially Anna, Brandon and baby William, whom Risa adored. All were healthy and happy; everything was wonderful.

"Hey, I haven't given you my present yet," Daniel whispered in her ear.

"Does it require privacy?" she inquired, her heart picking up a little as it always did when he was close.

"I think so. Let's go in for a moment. We can use the study."

He didn't have to ask twice. She was up and making her way across the yard with him. When he closed the door on the study, she jumped into his arms, hardly able to wait.

She ran her hands down his chest and lower, feeling him suck in a breath, hardening. Her voice was mischievous.

"So, is this my present?"

"That's your present for later. I have something else for you now."

She pouted as he drew away, wondering what he could have for her that had to be given in private. He took out a box from behind the desk—a plain brown box, unwrapped.

"What is it?"

"Open it and see."

She approached the box, smiling at him curiously. He was always surprising her—what had he cooked up now?

But peeling back the cardboard flaps, her breath caught when she saw the picture of her parents lying on the top of a stack of envelopes and papers. Picking it up, she looked at it—then at Daniel. The picture was taken of the three of them, shortly after Risa was born.

"Where? I thought these had all been lost."

"Laslow had them hidden in his collection of information about your family—he'd taken everything he could in his obsession with you all, seeing it as part of his 'work.' It took some doing, but I convinced Jack that this was all rightfully yours. There are some letters your parents wrote to each other before they were married, some things they wrote to you, too—apparently your mom had one of those journals where you keep track of things and write entries for your kids to look at later."

Risa was overwhelmed as she picked carefully through the box. She sat down at the desk, her knees shaking. She held the most precious of all things in her hands. The journal had a marker. She opened it, looked at the date and felt her chest tighten—it was the last entry her mom would have made before her death.

She read aloud to Daniel, her voice hoarse with emotion.

Dear Risa,

It's been a difficult day. Your father and I haven't had much time together lately, and all either of us wants is time with you, and with each other. We've been thinking about quitting the agency, leaving and trying to have a real life, a normal family, so that you can grow up and have a regular life. It's what we've always wanted for you. Our powers should always be used for good, but perhaps it's gone too far, and no one has the right to load such responsibility on a child. Should you choose to work for the good of mankind someday, that will be your choice, but I won't see your childhood stolen from you, as some of it already has been. We have to be careful out in the world, it's true, but life is a risk, and we all deserve the choice to live it as we see fit. Hopefully, it will all work out, and you'll be reading this thinking how silly I am, because your life is just fine. I hope so. We love you, baby. Be happy, Mom.

"Oh my God," Risa breathed out, the emotions nearly washing her away. She looked up at Daniel. "He had them killed because they were going to quit—they were going to take me away."

"Probably, but I think what she has to say there is more important, Risa. What they wanted—for each other, and for you. What you have now, a normal life. To be part of a loving family. It's come late, but you have it now."

"Your family has made me feel like they are my own, even if they're not."

"They can be. Look down at the bottom of the box."

What more could there be?

She reached down, finding a small black velvet box there, and looked at Daniel uncertainly. He took the box from her trembling fingers.

"It was your mother's. She requested her wedding ring stay on when she was buried, but her engagement ring was left to you. I had it reset—I hope you don't mind. I'd like it to be your engagement ring, Risa. Will you marry me?"

Risa looked at the beautiful ring as Daniel slid it on her finger, and felt everything inside of her settle. This was right; this was how it was supposed to be. But there were still complications. Daniel was still an agent, and she had no idea what she was going to do. The agency had invited her back, but she didn't think that was her path anymore. She didn't know if she could live with him disappearing off on dangerous missions. Could they ever have a normal life, really?

"Daniel, I want to marry you more than I can tell you, but how can we make it work, with your job? I don't know if I can—"

He shushed her gently. "I'm leaving the agency, Risa. No more of that for me. I want to come out of the shadows. I decided that weeks ago, but I've had a lot to do to wrap things up. I want to be here, with you. Though maybe not right here on the Cape."

"Where?"

"Ben and I have been talking about opening an investigation firm closer to the city—something high-tech, maybe surveillance. We thought you might be interested in a job?" His smile was mischievous as he teased her, and she slapped him playfully, laughing and slipping from the chair down into his arms.

"Well, that's quite an offer—marriage, a dog and a job. How can I say no?"

As his mouth found hers, he smiled. "My thoughts exactly."

* * * * *

Happily ever after is just the beginning...

Turn the page for a sneak preview of
DANCING ON SUNDAY AFTERNOONS
by
Linda Cardillo.

Harlequin Everlasting—Every great love
has a story to tell. ™
A brand-new line from Harlequin Books
launching this February!

Prologue

Giulia D'Orazio
1983

I had two husbands—Paolo and Salvatore.

Salvatore and I were married for thirty-two years. I still live in the house he bought for us; I still sleep in our bed. All around me are the signs of our life together. My bedroom window looks out over the garden he planted. In the middle of the city, he coaxed tomatoes, peppers, zucchini—even grapes for his wine—out of the ground. On weekends, he used to drive up to his cousin's farm in Waterbury and bring back manure. In the winter, he wrapped the peach tree and the fig tree with rags and black rubber hoses against the cold, his massive, coarse hands gentling those trees as if they were his fragile-skinned babies. My neighbor, Dominic Grazza, does that for me now. My boys have no time for the garden.

In the front of the house, Salvatore planted roses. The roses I take care of myself. They are giant, cream-colored, fragrant. In the afternoons, I like to sit out on the porch with my coffee, protected from the eyes of the neighborhood by that curtain of flowers.

Salvatore died in this house thirty-five years ago. In the last months, he lay on the sofa in the parlor so he could be in the middle of everything. Except for the two oldest boys, all the children were still at home and we ate together every evening. Salvatore could see the dining room table from the sofa, and he could hear everything that was said. "I'm not dead, yet," he told me. "I want to know what's going on."

When my first grandchild, Cara, was born, we brought her to him, and he held her on his chest, stroking her tiny head. Sometimes they fell asleep together.

Over on the radiator cover in the corner of the parlor is the portrait Salvatore and I had taken on our twenty-fifth anniversary. This brooch I'm wearing today, with the diamonds—I'm wearing it in the photograph also—Salvatore gave it to me that day. Upstairs on my dresser is a jewelry box filled with necklaces and bracelets and earrings. All from Salvatore.

I am surrounded by the things Salvatore gave me, or did for me. But, God forgive me, as I lie alone now in my bed, it is Paolo I remember.

Paolo left me nothing. Nothing, that is, that my

family, especially my sisters, thought had any value. No house. No diamonds. Not even a photograph.

But after he was gone, and I could catch my breath from the pain, I knew that I still had something. In the middle of the night, I sat alone and held them in my hands, reading the words over and over until I heard his voice in my head. I had Paolo's letters.

* * * * *

Silhouette®
ROMANTIC SUSPENSE

Excitement, danger and passion guaranteed!

Same great authors and riveting editorial you've come to know and love.

Look for our new name next month as Silhouette Intimate Moments® becomes Silhouette® Romantic Suspense.

Bestselling author Marie Ferrarella is back with a hot new miniseries— The Doctors Pulaski: Medicine just got more interesting....

Check out her first title, HER LAWMAN ON CALL, next month.

Look for it wherever you buy books!

This February...

Catch NASCAR Superstar **Carl Edwards** *in*

SPEED DATING!

Kendall assesses risk for a living—so she's the last person you'd expect to see on the arm of a race-car driver who thrives on the unpredictable. But when a bizarre turn of events—and NASCAR hotshot Dylan Hargreave—inspire her to trade in her ever-so-structured existence for "life in the fast lane" she starts to feel she might be on to something!

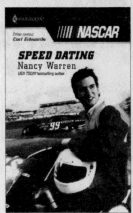

REQUEST YOUR FREE BOOKS!

2 FREE NOVELS PLUS 2 FREE GIFTS!

HARLEQUIN®

Blaze

Red-hot reads!

YES! Please send me 2 FREE Harlequin® Blaze® novels and my 2 FREE gifts. After receiving them, if I don't wish to receive any more books, I can return the shipping statement marked "cancel." If I don't cancel, I will receive 6 brand-new novels every month and be billed just $3.99 per book in the U.S., or $4.47 per book in Canada, plus 25¢ shipping and handling per book and applicable taxes, if any*. That's a savings of at least 15% off the cover price! I understand that accepting the 2 free books and gifts places me under no obligation to buy anything. I can always return a shipment and cancel at any time. Even if I never buy another book from Harlequin, the two free books and gifts are mine to keep forever.

151 HDN EF3W 351 HDN EF3X

Name	(PLEASE PRINT)
Address	Apt.
City	State/Prov.	Zip/Postal Code

Signature (if under 18, a parent or guardian must sign)

Mail to the **Harlequin Reader Service®:**
IN U.S.A.: P.O. Box 1867, Buffalo, NY 14240-1867
IN CANADA: P.O. Box 609, Fort Erie, Ontario L2A 5X3

Not valid to current Harlequin Blaze subscribers.

Want to try two free books from another line?
Call 1-800-873-8635 or visit www.morefreebooks.com.

* Terms and prices subject to change without notice. NY residents add applicable sales tax. Canadian residents will be charged applicable provincial taxes and GST. This offer is limited to one order per household. All orders subject to approval. Credit or debit balances in a customer's account(s) may be offset by any other outstanding balance owed by or to the customer. Please allow 4 to 6 weeks for delivery.

Your Privacy: Harlequin is committed to protecting your privacy. Our Privacy Policy is available online at www.eHarlequin.com or upon request from the Reader Service. From time to time we make our lists of customers available to reputable firms who may have a product or service of interest to you. If you would prefer we not share your name and address, please check here. ☐

HB07

HARLEQUIN®
Blaze™

COMING NEXT MONTH

#303 JINXED! Jacquie D'Alessandro, Jill Shalvis, Crystal Green
Valentine Anthology
Valentine's Day. If she's lucky, a girl can expect to receive dark chocolate, red roses and fantastic sex! If she's not...well, she can wind up with a Valentine's Day curse...and fantastic sex! Join three of Harlequin Blaze's bestselling authors as they show how three very unlucky women can end up getting *very* lucky....

#304 HITTING THE MARK Jill Monroe
Danielle Ford has been a successful con artist most of her life. Giving up the habit has been hard, but she's kicked it. Until Eric Reynolds, security chief at a large Reno casino, antes up a challenge she can't back away from—one that touches her past and ups her odds on bedding sexy Eric.

#305 DON'T LOOK BACK Joanne Rock
Night Eyes, Bk. 1
Hitting the sheets with P.I. Sean Beringer might have been a mistake. While the sex is as hot as the man, NYPD detective Donata Casale is struggling to focus on their case. They need to wrap up this investigation fast. Then she'll be free to fully indulge in this fling.

#306 AT HER BECK AND CALL Dawn Atkins
Doing It...Better!, Bk. 2
Autumn Beskin can bring a man to his knees. The steamy glances from her new boss, Mike Fields, say she hasn't lost her touch. But while he may be interested in more than her job performance, he hasn't made a move. Guess she'll have to nudge this fling along.

#307 HOT MOVES Kristin Hardy
Sex & the Supper Club II, Bk. 2
Professional dancer Thea Mitchell knows all the right steps—new job, new city, new life. But then Brady McMillan joins her Latin tango dance class and suddenly she's got two left feet. When he makes his move, with naughty suggestions and even naughtier kisses, she doesn't know what to expect next!

#308 PRIVATE CONFESSIONS Lori Borrill
What does a woman do when she discovers that her secret online sex partner is actually her real-life boss—the man she's been lusting after for two years? She goes for it! Trisha Bain isn't sure how to approach Logan Moore with the knowledge that he's Pisces47, only that she wants to make the fantasy a reality. Fast...

www.eHarlequin.com

HBCNM0107